Across six decades, 20 studio albums and thousands of all-out live performances, Bruce Springsteen has cemented his position in music history time and time again. Whether it's the stadium anthems of *Born in the U.S.A.*, the folk acoustic of *Nebraska*, or the reflective themes of his latest album, *Letter to You*, Springsteen is a master of heartland rock – his songs give a voice to the common man, to the disillusioned, and to those that society has forgotten.

This book celebrates Springsteen's life and career, from starting out on the New Jersey bar-band circuit to becoming one of the most celebrated and influential artists in the world. And, of course, Bruce wouldn't be The Boss without the one-and-only E Street Band – discover how these masterful musicians have helped Springsteen tell his story.

STEEN

Image Getty Images

BRUCE SPRINGSTEEN

Future PLC Quay House, The Ambury, Bath, BA1 1UA

Editorial
Author **Joel McIver**
Editor **Jacqueline Snowden**
Designer **Thomas Parrett**
Compiled by **Jacqueline Snowden & Andy Downes**
Senior Art Editor **Andy Downes**
Head of Art & Design **Greg Whitaker**
Editorial Director **Jon White**

Contributors
Dan Peel, Philippa Grafton, Sarah Bankes

Cover images
Shutterstock, Getty Images

Photography
All copyrights and trademarks are recognised and respected

Advertising
Media packs are available on request
Commercial Director **Clare Dove**

International
Head of Print Licensing **Rachel Shaw**
licensing@futurenet.com
www.futurecontenthub.com

Circulation
Head of Newstrade **Tim Mathers**

Production
Head of Production **Mark Constance**
Production Project Manager **Matthew Eglinton**
Advertising Production Manager **Joanne Crosby**
Digital Editions Controller **Jason Hudson**
Production Managers **Keely Miller, Nola Cokely,
Vivienne Calvert, Fran Twentyman**

Printed in the UK

Distributed by Marketforce, 5 Churchill Place, Canary Wharf, London, E14 5HU
www.marketforce.co.uk Tel: 0203 787 9001

Bruce Springsteen Second Edition (MUB4390)
© 2022 Future Publishing Limited

FUTURE
Connectors.
Creators.
Experience
Makers.

Future plc is a public
company quoted on the
London Stock Exchange
(symbol: FUTR)
www.futureplc.com

Chief executive **Zillah Byng-Thorne**
Non-executive chairman **Richard Huntingford**
Chief financial officer **Penny Ladkin-Brand**

Tel +44 (0)1225 442 244

Widely
Recycled

For press freedom
with responsibility

CONTENTS

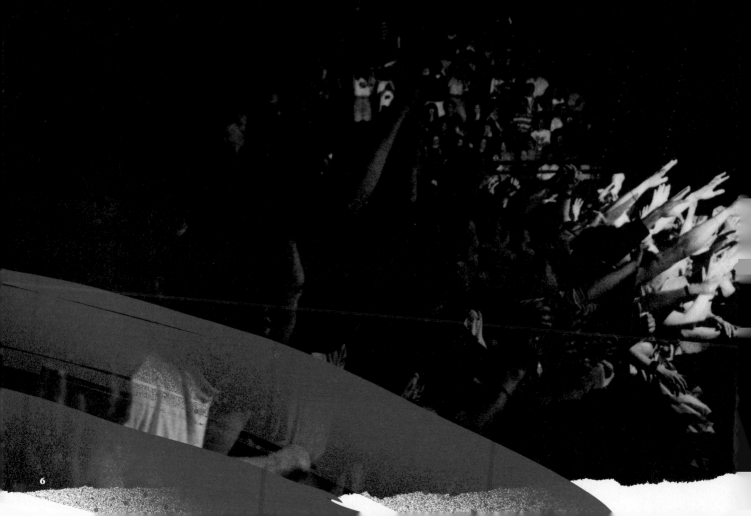

DISCOGRAPHY

CHAPTER 1
GROWIN' UP

DISCOGRAPHY 1973-1982

BOSS
IN WAITING

Before Bruce Springsteen found fame and fortune, he was just another kid with a guitar...

The new Bob Dylan? The voice of a disenfranchised generation? A spokesman for a particular American demographic? However you regard the work of Bruce Springsteen, it's rewarding to look back with a pinch of hindsight at his early life as a kid in New Jersey.

Springsteen's heritage is the classic East Coast USA blend of lineages for his age group. Born Bruce Frederick Joseph Springsteen in Long Branch, New Jersey, on 23 September 1949, he is of Dutch, Irish, and Italian descent – you only need to add Polish in there for the full house of European immigrant ancestry. His surname is a Dutch word that literally translates to 'leaping stone' but which more practically refers to a kind of European paving slab.

His father, Douglas, struggled to hold down a job and went through long periods of unemployment. Over the years he had taken on a variety of jobs, including factory worker, prison guard, and bus driver. He lived to the age of 73, dying in 1998 long after witnessing his son's rise to international fame. Springsteen's mother, Adele, was the family's main breadwinner, working as a legal secretary. At the time of writing, she is in her nineties, but was diagnosed with Alzheimer's in 2012. Springsteen has two younger sisters, Virginia and Pamela, the latter of whom later worked as an actor and photographer. Over the years he has rarely talked in

serious depth about his upbringing, with the obvious exception of his 2016 autobiography *Born to Run*: however, what cannot be underestimated is the importance of New Jersey to the worldview that he expresses in his music.

Evidence of the connection that Springsteen still has, even in his seventies, to the state of his birth can be seen throughout his career. In 2008, he was inducted into the New Jersey Hall of Fame, and he managed to encapsulate the grit and self-effacing sarcasm of the Garden State in the opening lines of his acceptance speech: "When I first got the letter I was to be inducted into the New Jersey Hall of Fame, I was a little

FAR LEFT The house on Institute Street in Freehold, New Jersey, where Bruce and his family lived from 1955 to 1962.

LEFT Springsteen with his mother, Adele, at the Grammy Awards in 2013.

suspicious. New Jersey Hall of Fame?… But then I ran through the list of names: Albert Einstein, Bruce Springsteen… my mother's going to like that. She's here tonight. It's her birthday and it's the only time she's going to hear those two names mentioned in the same sentence, so I'm going to enjoy it."

The Springsteens, a Catholic family, lived in South Street in the town of Freehold. Springsteen attended the St Rose of Lima Catholic School, and it was here that the first intellectual conflict of his life was felt. Like so many young religious men of his generation, too young to have fought in World War II but old enough to be ready for the rock'n'roll revolution, he found the doctrine imposed upon him by the nuns at school stifling. Still, he retained at least some affinity for the religion throughout his life, as he explained during an appearance at Monmouth University in New Jersey in 2017. "I was raised Catholic, and it informed my writing very deeply, and it continues to this day," he said. "There's simply nothing I can do about it. When I go to the creative well, many of the images and stories and the parables and the myths come up from inside me. I'm

> ## "WHEN I WAS GROWING UP, THERE WERE TWO THINGS THAT WERE UNPOPULAR IN MY HOUSE. ONE WAS ME, AND THE OTHER WAS MY GUITAR."
>
> ★★★★★ BRUCE SPRINGSTEEN

not very religious today, but if I see a priest, there's a glint in the two of our eyes."

Given the family's demographic, you can imagine that the swingin' tunes of the world's biggest star, New Jersey's own Frank Sinatra, were popular with both generations of the Springsteen household. However, a more muscular alternative to the slick crooning of Ol' Blue Eyes soon made itself heard with the advent of rock'n'roll music. A huge impact was made on the young Springsteen at the age of seven, when he witnessed the then red-hot Elvis Presley rocking the entire nation on *The Ed Sullivan*

Show, the entryway to the country's heart for many key musicians of the era. The impression on Springsteen was sufficient for him to request a guitar from his parents – a request which they granted, renting an instrument at the princely sum of six dollars a week – but at that point, he didn't stick with it.

That commitment came later, when The Beatles' epoch-shaping appearances on *The Ed Sullivan Show* in 1964 galvanised a whole continent of teenage rock stars-in-waiting. Much has been written about the influence of those Fab Four performances, coming

as they did just in time to enthuse a nation shocked by the recent assassination of President John F Kennedy and shaken by the bloody conflicts of the Vietnam War. There's no doubt that Bruce Springsteen, among thousands of his countrymen, was propelled to pick up a guitar in earnest after seeing those episodes of *Sullivan*. Our man, then 15 and at least some of the way towards his first flush of creativity, bought his second guitar at a local appliance store and set his heart on mastering it.

Within a year Springsteen was writing songs and performing in a band, The Rogues, at local venues such as the Elks Lodge in Freehold. His passion for music had overtaken everything else: teachers later reminisced that he was a "loner who wanted nothing more than to play his guitar". He remained with that band, about whom details remain scarce, for two years, while also playing with a second local group, The Castiles. The music in both outfits was similar to the surf and garage hybrid of the day, and Springsteen's young lyrics may or may not have been influenced by Bob Dylan, then approaching his imperial period.

In fact, Dylan remained a slightly touchy subject for Springsteen for some years after he became famous – say, from 1974 onwards – partly because the press endlessly compared the two musicians. "Dylan influenced me as much as anyone, I guess… when I was 14, maybe… but I don't think

TOP LEFT The press would often draw comparisons between Bruce Springsteen and fellow songwriter Bob Dylan.

TOP RIGHT Springsteen's yearbook photo, taken circa 1966. Springsteen did not enjoy his school years, preferring to focus on his music.

ABOVE The Beatles' famous 1964 US TV debut on *The Ed Sullivan Show* inspired Springsteen to buy a guitar.

Images Getty Images, Alamy (yearbook)

13

TOP The Stone Pony in Asbury Park, where Springsteen would often jam with other bands.

ABOVE When he was starting out, Springsteen was a frequent fixture in the music venues around Asbury Park. He later reflected on the area in the track '4th of July, Asbury Park (Sandy)'.

RIGHT Springsteen performed in several bands before The E Street Band came to be.

about the comparison too much," said Springsteen in a much-quoted interview with the writer Jerry Gilbert of *ZigZag* in August 1974.

In 1967 Springsteen graduated from Freehold High School, although he is said to have avoided the ceremony because he disliked school so much. Fortunately, he was not drafted to go to Vietnam, failing the physical examination after finishing high school. He had been concussed in a motorbike accident two years previously, and made a point of acting in an unstable manner at the draft examination, thus avoiding a potentially fatal trip to the jungle. A stint at Ocean County College proved short-lived, and a routine of playing in

more or less unsuccessful bands became his everyday norm.

Imagine the scene. It's the Summer of Love in America, and while San Francisco is suffused with lysergic love and the hippies are handing out flowers in the sunshine, in New Jersey the vibes are cold and grey. Of course, the fact that New Jersey is immediately adjacent to New York City, a world-class nexus of art and music only equalled by Los Angeles and London, doesn't help: New Jersey has always been NYC's insecure sibling in that sense. The entire Springsteen family upped and moved to San Mateo, California in 1969, leaving only Bruce and his sister Virginia – who had recently married – behind.

"I just read an article in the newspaper that says that New Jersey remains the number one state that people move away from!" laughed Springsteen in 2017. "After all my hard work… but I made my living writing about moving away from New Jersey, so maybe that has something to do with it."

This is the key to any understanding of Bruce Springsteen's early years: that New Jersey, one of the least glamorous states in the Union, had a certain raw appeal that not only caused him to remain there while others moved on to pastures new, it also informed his music to a profound degree. In the Rogues and Castiles years, he gritted his teeth and refused to give up, writing his

Images Getty Images, Alamy (Asbury Park)

LEFT Channelling one of his idols: "Everything starts and ends with Elvis. He wrote the book."

FAR RIGHT Springsteen and Steven Van Zandt on stage together in 1975. Van Zandt was also a member of some of Bruce's earlier bands.

RIGHT Springsteen first met saxophonist (and future E Street Band member) Clarence Clemons in 1971.

first songs, learning how to front a band and growing as a songwriter with every step forward he took.

From 1968 to 1969 Springsteen played in a band called Earth. It's amusing to consider that there was a contemporaneous British band of the same name that went on to become Black Sabbath. What's more, both Earths came from an environment of cultural poverty and shared a similarly pensive worldview. New Jersey's Earth was essentially a power trio before the concept of such a line-up had fully formed, with Springsteen backed by bassist John Graham and drummer Michael Burke.

In 1969, as Springsteen turned 20 years old, he made important connections with drummer Vini Lopez and organist Danny Federici, who remained his musical collaborators for some time to come. Forming a new band called Child with them, which quickly changed its name to Steel Mill, Springsteen began to stretch himself as a songwriter, aided by the talents of real musicians. One of these, guitarist Steve Van Zandt, became his best known collaborator, and remains so to this day.

Steel Mill lasted until January 1971, a miraculously long career for the era and the capricious nature of young musicians. The group's final line-up comprised Springsteen on vocals and guitar, backed by Federici and Lopez, as well as a second singer called Robbin Thompson and van Zandt on bass. Although Springsteen didn't release his first album for another two years, he and his bandmates truly earned their stripes as a live band, playing venues in and out of state and honing a defiantly uncompromising act.

The future was beckoning for our man, although – as we'll see – he had more than a few significant hurdles to overcome before stability finally came his way. The small matter of incessant poverty, and a workload that would level any lesser musician, were first and foremost among them.

"I HAD YOUTH, ALMOST A DECADE OF HARDCORE BAR BAND EXPERIENCE, A GOOD GROUP OF HOMEGROWN MUSICIANS... AND A STORY TO TELL."

★★★★ BRUCE SPRINGSTEEN
BORN TO RUN

BECOMING THE BOSS

How Bruce Springsteen evolved from a bar-band musician to one of the most famous rock stars on the planet

The story of Bruce Springsteen's rise from humble beginnings to his current status as one of the most important cultural figures of our time is a classic rock'n'roll tale. Like all such stories, it's all too easy to airbrush out the mundane details, romanticise the big picture and, in doing so, tell a story that is only partly true – so let's examine the bare facts.

The truth is that until 1971, Springsteen was just another talented kid from the New Jersey Shore. His musicianship was decent for a 22-year-old, and he certainly sang from the heart, but it took some serious industry allies to nurture that talent and bring it out – and what's more, he benefited hugely from the old-school record company model. Back then, and indeed until digital file-sharing killed profits from music around 2010, an artist was allowed to take their time about getting good – maybe over a few years and a bunch of albums. This was very much the case with Springsteen, who arguably hit peak form with his third record, 1975's *Born to Run*.

The industry mentors who saw the potential in the kid from Jersey were John Hammond, the renowned industry talent-spotter who had brought Bob Dylan to the Columbia label in the early Sixties, and that label's boss Clive Davis. Once Springsteen had signed on the dotted line with Columbia, it's fair to say that Davis and his team expected their boy to 'do a Dylan' and write some heartfelt acoustic songs.

LEFT Springsteen never felt particularly comfortable being touted as the 'future of rock'n'roll'.

BELOW 7 1/2 West End Court in Long Branch, New Jersey, where Springsteen wrote *Born to Run*.

While those influences are certainly audible on his 1973 debut album *Greetings from Asbury Park, N.J.*, the high points of the LP – which didn't exactly break commercial sales records – were the full-band songs recorded with a talented group of friends, The E Street Band. These musicians called him 'The Boss', even at this early stage, partly because he was their bandleader, partly because he used to collect and distribute their pay after gigs – and, although this may be an urban myth, because he used to dominate their backstage games of Monopoly.

Critics lined up to compare Springsteen with Dylan, predictably and tiresomely, an image he failed to dispel with *The Wild, the Innocent & the E Street Shuffle*, also released in '73 to indifferent sales. Still, the LP did yield the classic 'Rosalita (Come Out Tonight)' and introduced Springsteen's fans to 'his sound' – a hectic, soul-rock hybrid based on guitars and saxophone, with lyrics about cars, doomed love, nostalgia and the rigours of working-class life.

A famous if overblown quote by *Real Paper* critic Jon Landau – who wrote in 1974 "I saw rock and roll future, and its name is Bruce Springsteen. And on a night when I needed

"MY BUSINESS IS SHOW BUSINESS AND THAT'S THE BUSINESS OF SHOWING, NOT TELLING. YOU DON'T TELL PEOPLE ANYTHING. YOU SHOW THEM AND LET THEM DECIDE."

BRUCE SPRINGSTEEN
ON BEING TOUTED AS 'THE FUTURE OF ROCK AND ROLL', *BORN TO RUN*

MAIN At London's Hammersmith Odeon in 1975 – Springsteen and The E Street Band's first gig outside of America.

BELOW Van Zandt and Springsteen during a radio interview in 1976.

October 27, 1975 / 75 cents

Newsweek

Making Of A Rock Star

Bruce Springsteen

75 CENTS

OCTOBER 27, 1975

TIME

Rock's New Sensation

Bruce Springsteen

to feel young, he made me feel like I was hearing music for the very first time" – drew serious attention to the boy wonder, and he responded the following year with the fantastic *Born to Run*, by which time Landau had (uncoincidentally) become his manager.

Spending 14 months on his magnum opus, thanks to a giant wedge of budget advanced to him by Davis, Springsteen channelled everything he had into the fantastic title track and other soon-to-be-classics, such as 'Thunder Road' and 'Tenth Avenue Freeze-Out'. The E Street Band now prominently featured guitarist Steve Van Zandt, who became Springsteen's foil for the rest of his career – although, ironically, Van Zandt later became much more famous outside the music world as an actor, with a major role in HBO's *The Sopranos*.

The moment had come, and *Born to Run* made its 25-year-old creator a major star. Radio loved the new songs; magazines such as *Newsweek* and *Time* put him on their covers; and even a legal tussle with his then-manager Mike Appel couldn't do more than delay his ascendancy. Perhaps this stratospheric progress wore thin after a while for this most cerebral of songwriters, which explains the subtler, more introspective songs on *Darkness on the Edge of Town* in 1978. The songs were tighter and more considered, and Springsteen was enunciating his vocals with care as well as passion. A long US tour consolidated his position, with the long, fiery shows making Springsteen one of the major concert draws of the late Seventies.

Musicians now flocked to record Springsteen's songs. Manfred Mann's Earth Band scored a US number-one hit with 'Blinded By The Light', Patti Smith achieved

ABOVE A contact strip taken during a tour of the West Coast US, 1978.

TOP RIGHT After the breakthrough success of *Born to Run*, Bruce made the covers of both *Newsweek* and *Time* in the same week.

ABOVE RIGHT On stage at the Palladium in New York, October 1976.

RIGHT Springsteen has always had an intuitive ability to connect with his audience when performing live.

LEFT Signing autographs for fans after a concert in Birmingham, UK, during The River Tour.

ABOVE Taking a bow with The E Street Band, L-R: Clemons, Springsteen, Tallent, Federici, Weinberg, Van Zandt and Bittan.

great success with Springsteen's unreleased 'Because the Night', and The Pointer Sisters were highly acclaimed for their take on the previously unheard song 'Fire'. Most notably, Springsteen wrote four songs for his fellow Jersey Shore musicians Southside Johnny & The Asbury Jukes.

The singer's political convictions, now a well-known part of his legacy, began to make themselves heard around this time: in September 1979, Springsteen and The E Street Band recorded songs for the anti-nuclear power album, *No Nukes*. He continued to write songs with more or less direct political commentary in his evocation of poverty-stricken life in working-class America on the 1980 album *The River*, although the record also gave the world his first lightweight pop hit, 'Hungry Heart'. *The River* became Springsteen's first number-one hit on the Billboard chart, establishing him for the new decade.

A genius move came two years later with *Nebraska*, an acoustic solo album recorded on a portable four-track studio. The story goes that Springsteen had demoed the songs with the intention of teaching them to The E Street Band and recording full-band versions, but that their stark, personal nature made them more suitable to the solo treatment. Remember, this was a decade before the *MTV Unplugged* concept, and it took courage to experiment with the rock audience in such a way – but Springsteen's idea paid off, and *Nebraska* was widely hailed. *Rolling Stone* made the record its Album Of The Year, which might not sound like much until you remember that by 1982, punk rock had arrived, leaving a permanent stamp of

uncoolness on so-called 'rock dinosaurs' of the previous decade. The fact that Bruce Springsteen could not only survive this drastic sea change but thrive afterwards was testament to the honesty and staying power of his music.

In any case, any such speculation about Springsteen's rightful place in the post-punk Eighties was rendered instantly irrelevant

in 1984 when he released *Born in the U.S.A.*, which sold 15 million copies in the States and a further 30 million worldwide. One of the best-selling albums of all time, the record – and in particular, its highly ambiguous title track – inspires discussion to this day. Was he being patriotic or critical with the lyrics, which didn't specify his intentions in either direction? It's a conversation very similar to

LEFT The Boss, The Big Man, and Little Steven performing in Detroit, Michigan during The River Tour in 1981.

MAIN Raising his guitar to acknowledge the crowd during a concert, circa 1978.

Images Getty Images

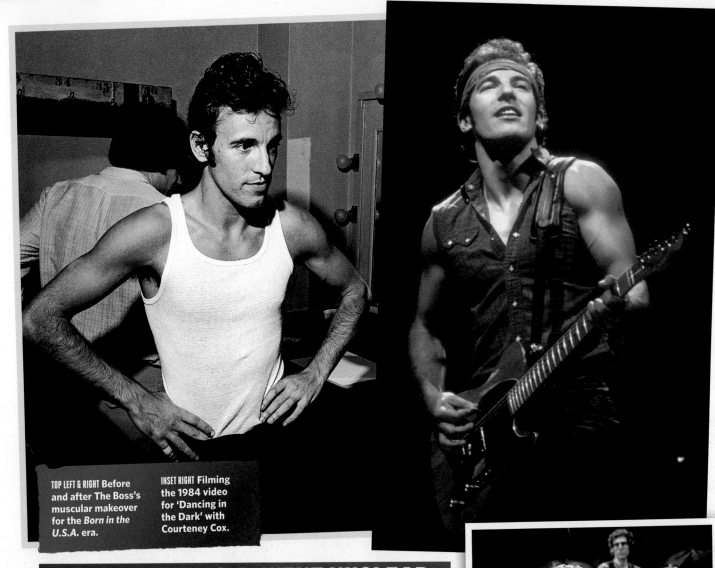

TOP LEFT & RIGHT Before and after The Boss's muscular makeover for the *Born in the U.S.A.* era.

INSET RIGHT Filming the 1984 video for 'Dancing in the Dark' with Courteney Cox.

"BORN IN THE U.S.A. WENT NUCLEAR... IT'S ALWAYS A BIT OF A MYSTERY WHEN SOMETHING BREAKS THAT BIG."

BRUCE SPRINGSTEEN
BORN TO RUN

that sparked 14 years previously when the late Jimi Hendrix played a ragged version of 'The Star-Spangled Banner' at Woodstock.

Springsteen did offer some clarity later that year after the then-President, Ronald Reagan, said at a rally, "America's future rests in a thousand dreams inside your hearts. It rests in the message of hope in the songs of a man so many young Americans admire – New Jersey's own Bruce Springsteen." This sugary nonsense was swiftly dismissed by the singer, who told a live audience shortly afterwards: "I kind of got to wondering what [Reagan's] favourite album of mine must've been, you know? I don't think it was the *Nebraska* album. I don't think he's been listening to

this one," before playing 'Johnny 99', a song about poverty and crime among America's poorest communities.

More recently, Springsteen has discussed the appropriation of 'Born in the U.S.A.' as a patriotic anthem – coincidentally with another President, Barack Obama – on the pair's *Renegades* podcast: "It did demand of you to hold two contradictory ideas in your mind at one time; that you can both be very critical of your nation and very prideful of your nation simultaneously," he explained.

Even more so than *Born to Run*, the *Born in the U.S.A.* album defines Springsteen for many of his followers, not least because it spawned no fewer than seven hits. You couldn't escape Springsteen in the back half

of the Eighties, with MTV supporting his every move. A notable video was made for 'Dancing in the Dark', an almost ridiculously catchy song that stars Courteney 'Monica from *Friends*' Cox, cutting a rug with Springsteen. It's one of the defining images of the entire decade, just as Cox herself helped to define the decade that followed.

After this career high, and the *Live/1975-85* five-record box set that came out in 1986, Springsteen slowed down the pace a little. His album *Tunnel of Love* appeared in 1987 and was a contemplative body of work, perhaps because he was undergoing relationship problems at the time. If he was hoping to retreat a little from the public eye, then he was out of luck, because one of his

live concerts the following year went on to be labelled one of the most important such events of all time by various commentators.

This was a concert in East Germany on 19 July 1988, which is said to have been conceived by the then-dominant Soviet-ruled government in an attempt to give their young people a taste of the Western culture that they craved. The political situation was tense, as the Russian-spearheaded perestroika ('restructuring') concept was mere months away from toppling the structure of the entire Soviet bloc. Old-style communism was taking its last breaths when Springsteen and his band walked onto the stage that day, and it's arguable that the 300,000 kids who saw them play were attracted and empowered by Springsteen's message. His music, a blend of affection and criticism for his home country and by definition the concept of capitalism, is honest, like it or not, and may well have seduced those youths, fed up of an overbearing government and a lack of personal freedom.

This is just one example of how influential a cultural and political figure Springsteen had become. He also headlined the Human Rights Now! Tour for Amnesty International in '88, while Little Steven was busying himself with the Artists United Against Apartheid movement. These were people who had applied the lessons of 1985's Live Aid to issues of oppression, meeting with great success. They changed the world: how many musicians can make the same claim?

ABOVE The crowd at Springsteen's concert in East Berlin on 19 July 1988. The Boss' performance fanned the flames of change.

LEFT Lofgren, Clemons and Bruce on stage in Pontiac, Michigan during The Born in the U.S.A. Tour, 1985.

BELOW Not all Seventies artists' careers survived the Eighties, but Springsteen proved to be an exception.

Images Getty Images, Alamy (Berlin)

Released January 1973

GREETINGS FROM ASBURY PARK, N.J.

Overexcited, overplaying and overthinking it: how Bruce Springsteen's charming but flawed debut album blazed a trail for his later works

Just 22 years old when he began recording his first album, Bruce Springsteen had a lot to say on *Greetings From Asbury Park, N.J.* – even if, close to half a century later, it feels as if he didn't quite get it all out. Its nine songs are packed full of imagery, allegory and metaphors, with the lyrics passionate, vivid and not a little amateurish – but damn, it sounds so good.

Those nine songs began as seven. When Columbia Records boss Clive Davis – who had advanced the sum of $25,000 to Springsteen and his manager, Mike Appel, to record the album – heard an early version, he rejected it, feeling (accurately, in retrospect) that it lacked a hit single. Essentially told by his boss to go home and come back when he had a hit, Springsteen wrote 'Blinded by the Light' and 'Spirit in the Night', which do indeed sound more lively than most of the existing tracks. Davis

accepted the new music, fortunately, and so the album was released.

Dig into these decades-old songs, and they still sound vital and fresh. The hit-that-never-was, 'Blinded by the Light', sounds like a jam session between members of Van Morrison's band, all soulful saxophone stabs from Clarence Clemons and burbled skeins of words from the young bandleader. The same is true of 'Growin' Up', 'Does This Bus Stop at 82nd Street?', 'For You' and the album closer 'It's Hard to Be a Saint in the City' – which is not to say that they sound identical, by any means: simply that they share an upbeat energy and the sense of romantic yearning that crystallised in Springsteen's later years.

More subtle sounds can be enjoyed on the songs recorded solely as a trio: the album intentionally splits its running time between Springsteen as 'big band leader' and Springsteen as 'acoustic troubadour'. It's understandable, if slightly regrettable, that the critics – who, by and large, gave great reviews to *Greetings From Asbury Park, N.J.* – chose to focus on Bob Dylan comparisons when discussing these songs. Take 'Mary Queen of Arkansas', for example: given that it's largely made up of a lightly strummed acoustic guitar, tremulous, lovelorn vocals and a harmonica, it would have been hard for the reviewers *not* to have mentioned the D word. The same goes for 'The

Angel', which centres on a dramatic vocal performance and a piano.

Elsewhere, Springsteen delves into soulful, sub-Motown territory on the other new cut, 'Spirit in the Night', and a semi-dirge of the Leonard Cohen school in 'Lost in the Flood', in which our chap addresses the subject of returning Vietnam veterans. Here he enters the lyrical zone that we recognise from his later, better-known songs, invoking religious references and car metaphors, always two of his trademark tropes.

It's powerful stuff, marred slightly by youthful overexuberance, but as an opening statement of intent, Springsteen's debut album deserved all the praise it got. It didn't sell particularly well, but as the decades have passed, its significance as a chronicle of its era has been widely accepted.

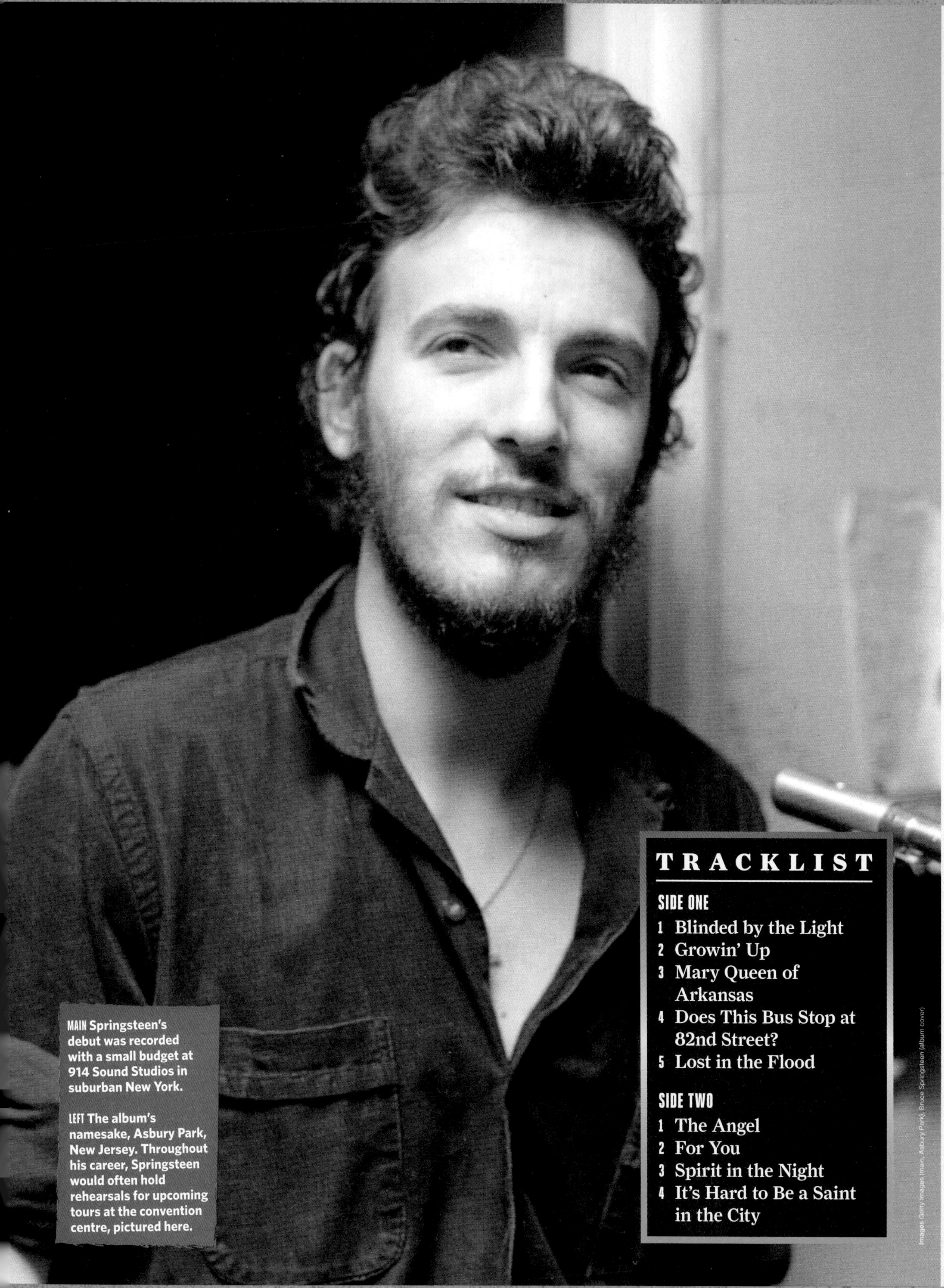

MAIN Springsteen's debut was recorded with a small budget at 914 Sound Studios in suburban New York.

LEFT The album's namesake, Asbury Park, New Jersey. Throughout his career, Springsteen would often hold rehearsals for upcoming tours at the convention centre, pictured here.

TRACKLIST

SIDE ONE

1 Blinded by the Light
2 Growin' Up
3 Mary Queen of Arkansas
4 Does This Bus Stop at 82nd Street?
5 Lost in the Flood

SIDE TWO

1 The Angel
2 For You
3 Spirit in the Night
4 It's Hard to Be a Saint in the City

Images Getty Images (main, Asbury Park), Bruce Springsteen (album cover)

Released November 1973

THE WILD, THE INNOCENT & THE E STREET SHUFFLE

With his second album, Bruce Springsteen allowed his ambition to break free of its former shackles – and unleashed a joyous suite of songs

Whatever was in the water supply at 914 Studios outside New York City from May to September 1973, we want some. The songs on *The Wild, the Innocent & the E Street Shuffle* are as long and vivid as its title, with four of the seven tracks taking up more than seven minutes of the listener's time – but they never feel too long. It seemed that Bruce Springsteen had hit a rich vein of inspiration, and we were the lucky ones who benefited from it.

Gone were the acoustic whimsies and mumbled lyrical overload of Springsteen's first album. On the new record, the opening song, 'The E Street Shuffle', kicked off with an unexpectedly unhinged brass introduction, before slipping seamlessly into a funk-rock hybrid that reminds the modern listener of Sheryl Crow, so laconic is its vocal delivery. At the back end of the track, the tempo speeds up for extra energy,

making the song one of Springsteen's most developed so far. This is followed by '4th of July, Asbury Park (Sandy)', a ballad in which the singer allows himself to slip into nostalgic romance with lines such as "And the boys from the casino dance with their shirts open, like Latin lovers on the shore." A recognisably Springsteen image, you'll agree.

What makes this album better than its predecessor is Springsteen's improved gauge of mood and dynamics. 'Kitty's Back' is a slow electric blues song with soul elements, and while that's a tad unexpected, it's standard fare compared to 'Wild Billy's Circus Story'. Inspired by memories of the travelling circus that used to come to Freehold each summer, Springsteen was clearly in the mood to experiment: tuba and accordion give the track the unhinged fairground edge that its title implies. While circus vibes aren't for everybody, they certainly give the album an unusual twist at its midpoint.

This album really comes into its own on its second side, with organ-driven power and a big, emotional chorus on 'Incident On 57th Street', before Springsteen's first true classic: 'Rosalita (Come Out Tonight)'. This fan favourite, with which he has often ended his live shows, displays arena-sized dynamics throughout. There are effortless stop-start moments from the band, a high emotional peak, whole-band shouts that

beg for audience participation – and the result is his first fully stadium-appropriate production. After that, the nine-minute 'New York City Serenade' seems relatively calm in comparison, with its piano, plaintive vocals and strings. It too rises and falls at least twice before fading away, leaving the listener deeply engaged and impressed.

Despite its many admirable qualities, this album didn't exactly sell in the millions – at least, not until Springsteen's profile took a leap into the stratosphere. That came soon enough, as we'll see…

TRACKLIST

SIDE ONE
1 The E Street Shuffle
2 4th of July, Asbury Park (Sandy)
3 Kitty's Back
4 Wild Billy's Circus Story

SIDE TWO
1 Incident on 57th Street
2 Rosalita (Come Out Tonight)
3 New York City Serenade

MAIN Springsteen's sophomore effort was released less than a year after his debut, but it failed to be a commercial breakthrough.

ABOVE RIGHT While E Street features in the album, the band would not formally become The E Street Band until September 1974.

RIGHT E Street in Belmar, New Jersey. The band used to rehearse on E Street in Sancious's mother's garage, inspiring their eventual name choice.

Images Getty Images, Bruce Springsteen (album cover)

Released August 1975

BORN TO RUN

The album that made Bruce Springsteen a superstar still stands strong today – and it was all down to a little six-note guitar lick...

Jon Landau, a critic who became Bruce Springsteen's manager, was at least partly responsible for the young singer's rise to glory in the mid-Seventies. His much-cited – and slightly ungrammatical – magazine quote from 1974, "I saw rock and roll future and its name is Bruce Springsteen," was used as a marketing slogan around the launch of *Born to Run*, although it should be noted that Springsteen himself disliked it. However, it helped to persuade CBS to stump up a large budget for the recording of the new album, a process that took 14 months: Springsteen was looking to replicate the 'Wall of Sound' production pioneered by producer Phil Spector, and while he achieved that goal to a degree, getting there wasn't easy. Matters weren't helped by conflicts between Landau and Mike Appel, as well as Springsteen's twin goals of improving his singing style and appealing to a wider audience by invoking fewer 'New Joisey' references.

The result is an album stuffed with classics, from top to bottom. 'Thunder Road' kicks off in truly overblown style, and is pretty much solely responsible for the view of certain critics that Springsteen often strays too far into macho, shouty territory – an ironic development considering his relatively timid roots. A more charitable view would be that the song is uplifting, from the heart and full-throated when it comes to the vocal performance, bolstered by a guitar solo in unison with the saxophone. 'Night' and 'She's the One' share a similar vibe, with guitars far more present in the songwriting, and their interplay with Clarence Clemons' sax now a recognisable trademark of Springsteen's music.

Elsewhere, Springsteen takes his foot off the gas, exploring different textures. Take 'Tenth Avenue Freeze-Out', a strings- and piano-driven production. The vocals are far more operatic than on the previous two albums, almost as if Springsteen had made a conscious decision to abandon a nasal style and sing from his diaphragm for the first time. Roy Orbison's singing style comes to mind here, but not so much in the two most ballad-esque songs: 'Backstreets' and 'Meeting Across the River'. The album's last song, 'Jungleland', begins with a strings introduction, enters an ascending chord sequence and builds towards a climax at six minutes in, before a more downbeat outro. Springsteen's vision was evident here, as well as the chunky budget given to him by corporate paymasters.

This just leaves the small matter of the title track, easily Springsteen's biggest ever song alongside 1984's 'Born in the U.S.A.'. Little Steven co-wrote – or wrote, depending on which source you consult – the sparkling, six-note guitar line that anchors this song of love, desperation and the "runaway American dream," and like the superpowered vehicles that populate the lyrics, the song motors forward persuasively. It was an obvious hit, and its legacy is huge, perhaps because its tone is so heartfelt, so lovelorn and so very much a passionate cri de coeur: the primal scream of star-crossed lovers confronted with the grim, grey machine of America's industrial core.

Has Springsteen ever bettered this song? For fans of a certain generation, absolutely not. Little wonder that the *Born to Run* album has gone on to sell six million copies, reached number three on the US album charts, and earned its creator, now a bona fide star, a whole shelf-load of gold and platinum awards. With this album, Bruce Springsteen had finally arrived.

TRACKLIST

SIDE ONE
1 Thunder Road
2 Tenth Avenue Freeze-Out
3 Night
4 Backstreets

SIDE TWO
1 Born to Run
2 She's the One
3 Meeting Across the River
4 Jungleland

MAIN *Born to Run* was seen as Springsteen's last chance for a commercial hit record – safe to say it paid off.

TOP LEFT Some six months of the recording process was spent on 'Born to Run', as The Boss initially struggled to convey his ideas.

ABOVE LEFT Bruce pictured in July 1975 during a mammoth 19-hour rehearsal session for the Born to Run Tour.

NOVEMBER 1975
A characteristically energetic performance from Springsteen alongside Clemons, Federici and Van Zandt while in Amsterdam during the Born To Run Tour.

★ ★ ★ ★

32

Released June 1978

DARKNESS ON THE EDGE OF TOWN

Springsteen's first truly mature album saw him embrace late-Seventies hard rock, while focusing on the heartlands of his youth

Getting famous isn't for everybody, as Bruce Springsteen found out after the enormous success of *Born to Run*. Fame simply wasn't enough for him – as he later explained, he specifically wanted to be great at his art. Perhaps that explains the more introverted, pensive nature of the songs on *Darkness on the Edge of Town*, which embrace a more thoughtful vibe while amping up the chart-friendly melodies.

Nowhere is this evolution more obvious than on the first song, 'Badlands', which has an immediately catchy set of hooklines all over its instrumentation, as well as a confidence and swagger that shows exactly where Springsteen's head was at in the era of punk rock. The piano is thudding; the guitars are beefed up with overdrive; and Springsteen's vocals are loaded once more with Roy Orbison-style power vibrato. Little Steven, an increasingly important member of The E Street Band, was given a co-production credit on this album for

his help with arranging the songs – and if you want an example of an effective arrangement, look no further than the dramatic breakdown and rebuild at three minutes into the song, almost shamelessly designed for stadium crowds.

If we're completely honest, to modern ears, songs like this – plus 'Something in the Night' and 'Streets of Fire', classics though they undoubtedly are – verge on being over the top, with rather too much pomposity when a touch of subtlety would have been welcome. Yes, these compositions work perfectly when you see them performed live – on record, however, that's a whole of earnest bellowing and honking sax for the listener to take in. Of course, this is essentially blasphemy for the Bruce devotee, but read on.

The great thing about this album, and its redeeming feature, is that Springsteen appears to be totally aware of his tendency to overdo things, and backs off a long way for the more tender songs, of which there are many. Take 'Adam Raised a Cain', for example, which has a slightly jarring reggae and soul feel and where the vocals are genuinely harsh at points – this is appropriate, as it's about a dysfunctional father and son relationship. This theme explains its appearance in a 2014 episode of the TV series *Sons of Anarchy*, itself a *Hamlet*-inspired drama. 'Candy's Room',

too, addresses the theme of prostitution, encapsulated in a piano line that escalates to a 'Born to Run'-style upbeat anthem.

In case this all sounds like heavy going, take solace in the gorgeous ballad 'Racing in the Street', which distils all of Springsteen's obsessions – muscle cars, the long-lost America of the Fifties and Sixties, and doomed love – into a single composition. You'll find 'The Promised Land' and 'Factory' both heartfelt and thoughtful, and there's also the whimsical 'Prove It All Night'. The album ends with its title track, a massive composition anchored by a hefty piano and bass groove, in which Springsteen tells the tale of a loser who refuses to give up.

This is a multifaceted album that asks big questions of the listener, and critics gave it a medium-warm reception as a result, perhaps unsure how to take it. Nowadays it's regarded as a classic, in part thanks to a sustained reissue campaign in 2009, when it was remastered and expanded with demo and bootleg tracks.

BELOW LEFT Several tracks originally intended for *Darkness* became hits for other artists: Patti Smith (pictured) added her own lyrics to an unfinished 'Because the Night', while 'Fire' was made famous by The Pointer Sisters.

MAIN On stage in 1978. More than four decades on, *Darkness* is widely regarded as one of Springsteen's finest albums.

TRACKLIST

SIDE ONE
1 Badlands
2 Adam Raised a Cain
3 Something in the Night
4 Candy's Room
5 Racing in the Street

SIDE TWO
1 The Promised Land
2 Factory
3 Streets of Fire
4 Prove It All Night
5 Darkness on the Edge of Town

Images Getty; Images: Bruce Springsteen (album cover)

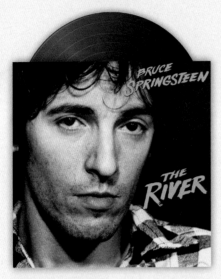

Released October 1980

THE RIVER

In the Eighties, the era of Duran Duran and hip-hop, would Bruce Springsteen triumph – or would be up The River without a paddle?

In 1979, Bruce Springsteen was enjoying a burst of serious songwriting inspiration. Planning a follow-up to *Darkness on the Edge of Town* for release, he originally came up with 50 songs – and attempted to cherry-pick a single LP from them. Failing to do so satisfactorily, he arranged a double album instead, his only such release to date.

Now, as most of us know, double albums are almost invariably made up of a great single LP plus inessential filler, and while that's not exactly the case with *The River* –

an immense achievement, and pivotal in Springsteen's career – there are songs here that haven't stood the test of time as well as others. This is exacerbated by the fact that our man was in a retrospective mood, enjoying the lightweight rock'n'roll sounds of his youth as much as the heavyweight songwriting of his heyday, and for that reason certain tracks sound a little flippant. Let's name them and get them out of the way: the prime culprits are 'Sherry Darling', 'Crush on You', 'You Can Look (But You Better Not Touch)', 'Cadillac Ranch', 'I'm a Rocker' and 'I Wanna Marry You', the last of these as saccharine as its title would suggest.

However, there are 20 songs on this behemoth of a record, and so there's plenty of profundity to enjoy once the lesser tracks are dispensed with. 'Hungry Heart' was the big hit: it's an unashamedly cheesy pop anthem, with Springsteen's voice sped up during production, hence its slightly

unfamiliar tone. The song was originally written for The Ramones, but manager Jon Landau persuaded Springsteen to issue it himself – a canny move, as it was a worldwide success. More serious themes were addressed in 'Independence Day' – a leftover tune from the *Darkness* album, and a plangent tale of father and son conflict – and of course 'The River' itself. This harmonica-laden song, in which Springsteen's cowboy drawl of "I got a job working construction, for the Johnstown Company / but lately there ain't been much work, on account of the economy," supplies his perspective on the social conditions of the day.

It's fascinating to hear how Springsteen has absorbed some lessons from the post-punk and New Wave artists of the day: listen out for the upbeat 'Ramrod' and 'The Price You Pay', plus the one-finger keyboard line in the energetic 'Jackson Cage' and a similar hook in 'Two Hearts', where his voice reaches

TRACKLIST

SIDE ONE
1 The Ties That Bind
2 Sherry Darling
3 Jackson Cage
4 Two Hearts
5 Independence Day

SIDE TWO
1 Hungry Heart
2 Out in the Street
3 Crush on You
4 You Can Look (But You Better Not Touch)
5 I Wanna Marry You
6 The River

SIDE THREE
1 Point Blank
2 Cadillac Ranch
3 I'm a Rocker
4 Fade Away
5 Stolen Car

SIDE FOUR
1 Ramrod
2 The Price You Pay
3 Drive All Night
4 Wreck on the Highway

MAIN *The River* became Springsteen's first album to top the Billboard charts.

RIGHT He's a rocker: on stage with Clemons in Los Angeles, 1981.

TOP RIGHT Photos of Bruce and the band that featured in *The River*'s album sleeve.

the very edges of its range. There's a very singable 'aye-aye-aye' chorus and some gorgeous 12-string guitars in the uptempo 'The Ties That Bind', and an interesting, interwoven vocal interplay in 'Out In The Street', too: clearly Springsteen was up to his eyes in ideas.

You'll also enjoy the quieter songs on *The River*, which include 'Point Blank' and 'Fade Away', both understated love ballads; 'Stolen Car', a very slight song with shimmering textures that explores the human search

for meaning; the even slighter 'Drive All Night', eight minutes of contemplation; and 'Wreck on the Highway', a very downtempo end to the album. As always, Springsteen is looking for answers: why are we here, and where are we headed?

The critics and public loved *The River*, which ultimately went five times platinum. And yet in career terms, Bruce Springsteen was barely getting started…

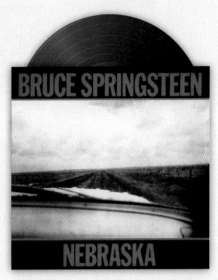

Released September 1982

NEBRASKA

Surely a platinum-selling artist like Bruce Springsteen wouldn't record an acoustic demo and put it out as a proper album... would he?

Nebraska was either a very well planned, deeply considered marketing move, or a sheer fluke, a decision made on the spur of the moment that paid off in spades. Consider the following and make up your own mind on the matter.

In early 1982, Bruce Springsteen presented The E Street Band with a bunch of songs for his forthcoming sixth studio album. Recorded on a four-track Teac recorder, the songs consisted of Springsteen on acoustic guitar, dropping in harmonica, mandolin and a few other instrumental bits and bobs along the way. Stark, lo-fi and absolutely not what people had come to expect from the all-guns-blazing, big-band Boss at this point in his career, the new songs were hardly fit for release, not least because the sole copy was a cassette that Springsteen carried around in his pocket – no cassette box needed! – for a couple of weeks.

Or were they? On discovering that the new songs didn't quite work in the full, electric band format, Springsteen and his manager Jon Landau decided to issue them exactly as they were, with the benefit of some noise-reduction and a mastering session. Adding some sombre artwork and titling the new collection *Nebraska* after its most profound song, they created a masterpiece.

The basic sound is Springsteen's vocals, a strummed or fingerpicked acoustic guitar – although one song, 'Open All Night', features an amplified electric instrument – and a wailing harmonica line or two. The vibe ranges from country (the title cut), folk ('Johnny 99'), upbeat ('Open All Night'), to sheer bleakness ('My Father's House') and a kind of lo-fidelity grunge ('Reason to Believe') akin to Nirvana covering a Tom Waits murder ballad. Vocally, Springsteen varies his approach from a yee-haw drawl (the title song again) to a more committed rock effort on a couple of songs, but for the most part he is restrained – and therefore highly emotive.

This is where *Nebraska* shines most – in the emotional, searching nature of Springsteen's lyrics. 'Nebraska' itself is the true story of a Bonnie & Clyde-type killer couple, while 'Highway Patrolman' is the tale of a police officer with conflicting loyalties to duty and family. 'State Trooper' and 'Open All Night' also deal with the complex themes of morality and its consequences, while the rest of the album reveals Springsteen's opaque musings on the big themes – love and death.

To this day, *Nebraska* is regarded as a great album, and rightly so. You could arguably state that the move to issue the demo songs was as important as the songs themselves. Remember, this was 1982, a decade before the *MTV Unplugged* phenomenon, and well before every electric rock star decided to reinvent themselves as an acoustic troubadour. Once again, Bruce Springsteen was way ahead of his time.

TRACKLIST

SIDE ONE
1 Nebraska
2 Atlantic City
3 Mansion on the Hill
4 Johnny 99
5 Highway Patrolman
6 State Trooper

SIDE TWO
1 Used Cars
2 Open All Night
3 My Father's House
4 Reason to Believe

MAIN For some tracks, Springsteen drew inspiration from historian Howard Zinn's book *A People's History of the United States.*

LEFT Due to its more solemn tone, *Nebraska* was the first album that Springsteen didn't take on tour.

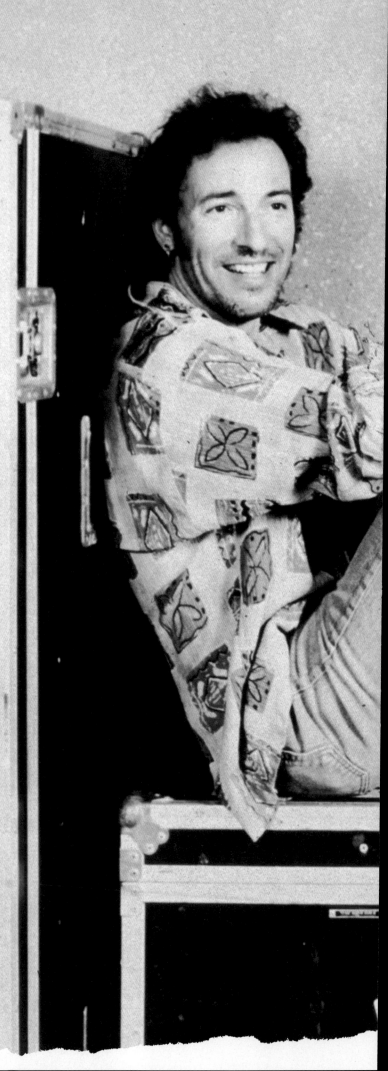

SIDE UP.

SPRINGSTEEN

JULY 1992

The Boss takes a break: Bruce puts his feet up amongst the equipment trunks backstage at New Jersey's Brendan Byrne Arena, during his 1992–1993 World Tour.

SIDE U

AN

CHAPTER 2
THE BOSS

42

DISCOGRAPHY 1984-1995

Images Getty Images

THE MUSICIAN

Is Bruce Springsteen a master musician, we hear you ask? The answer may surprise you...

When Bruce Springsteen became a teenager in late 1962, he did so at the very cusp of Beatlemania, and just before a global surge in enthusiasm for a brand-new form of music – rock'n'roll, later simplified as plain old rock. What a time to be picking up your very first instrument, right?

Now, as a budding guitarist, Springsteen's role models in the early rock years – say, before 1965 – would have been enthusiastic, R&B-influenced players. The Beatles, Keith Richards, Pete Townshend and the other early rock axemen were competent and imaginative, of course, but there were no genuine, lightning-fingered guitar heroes until the arrival of Eric Clapton, Jeff Beck and Jimi Hendrix in 1966 and '67. Jimmy Page, Ritchie Blackmore and Leslie West came to prominence soon after, and by 1970 the cult of the fleet-fingered soloist was permanently in place. Of course, this concept was taken to its logical conclusion a decade later by Eddie Van Halen, Randy Rhoads and the rest of the heavy metal shredders, but by then Springsteen was a bona fide rock star and probably paid little attention to their antics.

The big picture is that Springsteen attained his majority as a musician at an exact point in time, say 1971 to '73, when it was new and cool to be

a guitar demon. Eyewitnesses to his performances at this time in the bands Earth and Steel Mill – and there are a lot of them still around, both in and out of the music business – testify that Springsteen played like a true hotshot soloist back then. His influences were disparate, combining the speedy energy of surf bands such as The Ventures, slick pop along the lines of The Shadows, blues from Peter Green and all-round Americana of the type played so beautifully by John Fogerty. He also had a more mellow folk side, as we know, and indeed it was partly his grasp of

the acoustic guitar that first gained him attention from the record labels.

This is the key point: back in the pre-fame days, Springsteen was a master of fiery electric playing – among the finest of the Jersey Shore class of 1970, it's said. But when he streamlined his approach, recruited master musicians such as Stevie Van Zandt and focused instead on songwriting, he essentially *gave all that up*. That's an unprecedented move, as near as we can ascertain – to step away from instrumental histrionics and strip back to the core of what

LEFT Springsteen on his Takamine acoustic, at Wembley Stadium in July 1988.

ABOVE A typical high-octane Springsteen performance on stage in Los Angeles, 1994.

Images Getty Images

45

"ROCK'N'ROLL HAS BEEN EVERYTHING TO ME. THE FIRST DAY I CAN REMEMBER LOOKIN' IN THE MIRROR AND STANDIN' WHAT I WAS SEEIN' WAS THE DAY I HAD A GUITAR IN MY HAND."

★★★★★ BRUCE SPRINGSTEEN
SPEAKING TO *NEWSWEEK*, 1975

was and remains most important; in Springsteen's case, the dynamics and emotional heft of his songs.

In his autobiography, *Born to Run*, he wrote: "My voice was never going to win any prizes. The songs would have to be fireworks… the world was filled with plenty of good guitar players, many of them my match or better, but how many good songwriters were there?"

Still, anyone who has witnessed Springsteen in concert – at pretty much any point in his 50 years and counting as a live performer – will have borne witness to his lead and rhythm guitar playing. His solos, long and effortless despite the furrowed brow and serious demeanour that he adopts as he delivers them, focus on smooth, sweet vibrato, big string bends for expression, the occasional pinch harmonic and both legato and alternate picking. Translated for non-guitar nerds, that essentially means that he possesses the full range of blues and rock techniques, ornamenting his playing in expressive, emotional ways. He can still play like a bar-room bluesman, though: check out his anarchic, almost punk-rock guitar solo on Warren Zevon's 'Disorder in the House' in 2003.

As a songwriter, where do you go if you want a change of flavour from the guitar? To the piano, of course: it's the only other instrument that can replace a full band. This is because, like the guitar, it's capable of polyphony – in other words, playing more than one note at a time – which enables the player to nuance chords by making them major, minor, augmented, suspended or a myriad other variations. It's no surprise that Springsteen was writing songs on the piano from an early point in his career, although it's still an unexpected revelation that nearly all the songs on the *Born to Run* album were written on that instrument.

As with his guitar playing, and indeed the mandolin that he's been known to strap on from time to time, Springsteen's piano playing is strictly utilitarian – he uses the instrument to deliver subtle or strong chords that accompany his vocals, rather than flurries of notes that make the piano a feature. He plays well, of course, but not extravagantly, leaving that to other musicians in his band. Unlike his guitar playing, however, he never gained so much proficiency on the piano that it threatened his core objectives of songwriting and singing, obliging him to step back from that level of proficiency.

When it comes to Springsteen's third most commonly played instrument, the harmonica, he is far more lyrical, perhaps because the instrument is inherently expressive thanks to its limited note and tone ranges. Single-line melodies and slurred wails are his comfort zone, in the line of the blues heritage and the acoustic folkies that populated the Sixties and Seventies, from Bob Dylan to Tom Petty and beyond. True mastery at the level of Stevie Wonder or Toots Thielemans was never his objective or even within his

MAIN He's still got it: wowing the crowds at the 2009 Super Bowl halftime show.

BELOW Rehearsing with The E Street Band, circa 1978.

BOTTOM Axe and sax: Springsteen and Clemons rocking in Rome, Italy, 1988.

grasp, but then again, it didn't need to be. Just as he does with guitar and piano, Springsteen plunges his artistry into a few meaningful notes rather than many. See his heartfelt harmonica playing on *Born to Run*'s 'Thunder Road' and the title track of *The River* for evidence.

The lesson here is that Springsteen is a musician who prioritises message over medium. The heart of his songs is more important than their delivery, judging by his approach to the craft, although that is not to say that there aren't certain tried-and-tested methods that he uses in his songwriting in order to achieve a certain effect. As he once said, "Adult

47

MAIN On stage in Rotterdam, the Netherlands, during the 1992-1993 World Tour.

ABOVE With Lofgren and Van Zandt at Madison Square Garden in New York, 2016.

life is dealing with an enormous amount of questions that don't have answers, so I let the mystery settle into my music," which is a well-judged and ambiguous way of saying that his songs have a powerful effect on the listener that he would prefer not to explain.

We can do that for him by asking what it is he's trying to achieve with his songs. Springsteen wants us to understand the despair of poverty, the sadness of fragile or broken relationships, and the existential fear of a life spent in drudgery – and on the flipside, the adrenaline surge of new love, the empowerment of breaking through to freedom, and the sheer rush of forward motion. That's a whole lot of humanity to squeeze into

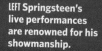

LEFT Springsteen's live performances are renowned for his showmanship.

BELOW The Boss bought his modified Fender electric guitar in 1973, and has been playing it for more than four decades.

a set of songs, but he elicits precisely those empathetic emotions in his listeners in a few simple ways.

First, he uses weighty sources for his lyrics – books, poems and songs that themselves evoke strong feelings – such as the Bible, John Steinbeck's *The Grapes of Wrath* and *East of Eden*, and the short stories and novels of Flannery O'Connor and James M Cain. Even if those sources aren't directly known to the listener, their influence still lends power. Then there's the deliberate continuity of his themes, one of those being a pair of star-crossed lovers who escape their bonds for the sake of their love: many of Springsteen's songs follow this theme, from 'Born to Run'

onward. In repeating and reinforcing this trope, Springsteen creates a whole world of his own, a world that his fans recognise and willingly engage with.

Finally, there are certain chord sequences that by their nature evoke anticipation or longing or tension, all essentially words for the same emotion in this context. Look at the dynamics of Springsteen's songs: sure, some are all mellow, or all upbeat, but the majority cover a wide range of territory. A popular Boss technique is to break down the instrumentation to its very essence towards the end of a song, so that only a guitar, drum or piano can be heard. He'll then intone and repeat a line, building in volume and intensity… until the whole

band rejoins on the turn of a dime, carrying the song – and the audience – to the final, triumphant chord. Songwriting like this can transform a song into a quasi-religious experience. Just ask any of the rapturous, tearful gig-goers who you see leaving one of his spellbinding shows.

Add to these tricks a breathtaking work ethic and the fact that he is among the greatest live performers in the business (Springsteen concerts are two parts adrenaline to three parts physical workout), and there's little wonder that as a musician and as a songwriter, Springsteen is one of the most successful, and fascinating, composers of our time.

Images Getty Images

"IF YOU JUST LOOKED AT THE OUTSIDE, IT'S PRETTY ALPHA MALE – YOU KNOW? WHICH IS A LITTLE IRONIC BECAUSE THAT WAS NEVER REALLY ME. I THINK I CREATED MY PARTICULAR STAGE PERSONA OUT OF MY DAD'S LIFE. AND PERHAPS I EVEN BUILT IT TO SUIT HIM TO SOME DEGREE."

★★★★★ BRUCE SPRINGSTEEN
ON HIS *BORN IN THE U.S.A.* STAGE PERSONA,
SPEAKING ON NPR'S *FRESH AIR*, 2016

RIGHT Springsteen in his famous 'work clothes' – the look he is arguably most associated with to this day.

Image Getty Images

INTRODUCING THE BAND

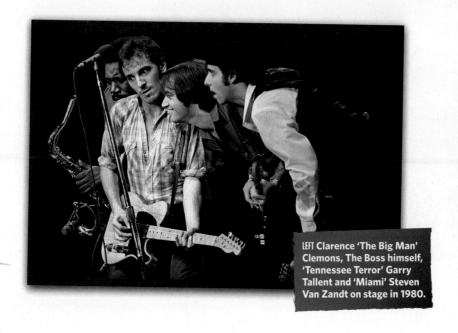

LEFT Clarence 'The Big Man' Clemons, The Boss himself, 'Tennessee Terror' Garry Tallent and 'Miami' Steven Van Zandt on stage in 1980.

How Mr Springsteen formed, disbanded and then re-formed the ultimate group of musicians...

Behind every successful star there's a supporting cast, as the received rock'n'roll wisdom goes, and the maxim definitely holds true in the case of Bruce Springsteen – whose E Street Band have become almost as widely known as their boss, or rather The Boss, himself. An outwardly motley crew whose relaxed, extroverted performances disguise musicianship of breathtaking quality, the group and their history are integral to any appreciation of Springsteen himself.

Where did these musicians come from? Like Springsteen himself, they had honed their skills around Asbury Park, where artists such as Southside Johnny, The Jaywalkers, The Sundance Blues Band and many more had competed with their future bandleader's early acts Earth and Steel Mill. As for their recording debut, the famous story goes that The E Street Band, who first gathered in October 1972, showed up to the recording of Springsteen's first album, 1973's *Greetings from Asbury Park, N.J.*, to the surprise of CBS Records, who were expecting him to deliver an album of acoustic protest balladry. Fortunately they stamped their mark on Springsteen's evolving sound, to the point where his next record, *The Wild, the Innocent & the E Street Shuffle* – also released in '73 – referenced what would soon be their official name.

Those first two records featured an early incarnation of the band, led by the visually and aurally dominant saxophonist Clarence Clemons and joined by bassist Garry Tallent, drummer Vini Lopez and two keyboard players, Danny Federici and David Sancious. It was the last of these who inspired the band's name, 1107 E Street being the house in Belmar, New Jersey, where Sancious' mother lived, and she would let the group practise in the garage. Thanks to the *Born to Run* song 'Tenth Avenue Freeze-Out', you'll see tourists searching in vain for this house at the intersection of E Street and 10th Avenue, but of course we know better.

Major developments came in 1974 and '75, just as Springsteen's profile was rising:

LEFT Clemons, Springsteen, Lofgren, Tallent and Scialfa during their Born in the U.S.A. Tour in 1984.

BELOW The band pictured with Ronnie Spector of The Ronettes (seated, centre) in 1976.

Lopez was replaced by Ernest 'Boom' Carter, although the latter didn't stay long; he was replaced in turn by the great Max Weinberg, who remains on Springsteen's drum stool to this day. Drum fans will appreciate the associated Weinberg factoid that his son Jay plays drums in the heavy metal band Slipknot, a rare example of parent and offspring achieving equal fame on the same instrument. Both men clearly value the Springsteen connection. Weinberg Senior once declared: "I will always desire to play with Bruce Springsteen. He's the most inspirational, most dedicated, most committed and most focused artist I've ever seen. I like to be around people like that."

Shortly after, keyboardist Roy Bittan and guitarist Steven Van Zandt – the latter dubbed 'Little Steven' – signed up, both long-standing E Streeters and the latter a very visible artist in his own right. In fact, the axeman quickly built a reputation as a master of stage and studio, and left in 1984 to strike out as a solo artist. His replacement that year was the virtuoso Nils Lofgren, and the band were also joined in '84 by

Springsteen's future-wife Patti Scialfa on vocals, and later guitar.

In concerts, Springsteen made a thoroughly enjoyable, highly theatrical spectacle out of announcing the band, introducing them with nicknames such as 'Professor' Roy Bittan, 'Miami' Steven Van Zandt and 'Mighty' Max Weinberg, before a huge welcome for the 'Big Man', Clarence Clemons. The last of these enjoyed a particularly devoted fanbase, explaining at one point: "As a horn player, the greatest compliment one can get is when a person comes to you and says, 'I heard this saxophone on the radio the other day and I knew it was you. I don't know the song, but I know it was you on sax'."

The other musicians soon became famous in their own right, and well-known artists began asking to work with them as the Eighties dawned. Tallent recruited Springsteen, Lofgren, Clemons and Weinberg for the Jersey Artists for Mankind band; Clemons and Lofgren toured as part of Ringo Starr's group; Bittan and Van Zandt recorded with Bob Dylan. Van Zandt also assembled the Artists United Against

Apartheid project, becoming the most visible E Street Band alumnus in doing so. Years later, he revealed that when dealing with warring factions in South Africa, he had dissuaded one particularly aggressive group from planning the assassination of Paul Simon, believe it or not.

The good times couldn't last forever, it seemed, and in 1989 Springsteen decided not to use The E Street Band musicians any more. This didn't lead to too much friction – he'd always paid them well and fairly, it's thought, and their friendships went back a long way – and besides, the

RIGHT The band performing at New York City's Shea Stadium during The Rising Tour in 2003.

★ NILS LOFGREN

★ STEVEN VAN ZANDT

★ ROY BITTAN

★ VINI LOPEZ

★ PATTI SCIALFA

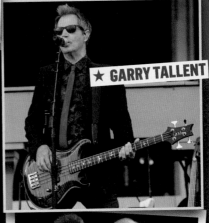

★ GARRY TALLENT

★ CLARENCE CLEMONS

★ DAVID SANCIOUS

★ DANNY FEDERICI

★ MAX WEINBERG

"A REAL ROCK'N'ROLL BAND EVOLVES OUT OF A COMMON PLACE AND TIME. IT'S ALL ABOUT WHAT OCCURS WHEN MUSICIANS OF SIMILAR BACKGROUND COME TOGETHER IN A LOCAL GUMBO THAT MIXES INTO SOMETHING GREATER THAN THE SUM OF ITS PARTS."

★★★★★ BRUCE SPRINGSTEEN
BORN TO RUN

FAR LEFT Audiences loved the interplay between The Boss and The E Street Band, particularly the relationship between Bruce and Clarence.

LEFT The 1999-2000 Reunion Tour marked the first time in over a decade that Springsteen and the band had regularly performed together.

MAIN The E Street Band's performance at the 2009 Super Bowl Halftime show was watched by almost 100 million people.

band members were in serious demand thanks to him. Tallent became a producer in Nashville, Lofgren and Clemons went solo, and Weinberg considered a career as a lawyer, although he ultimately chose to remain a musician, notably on *Late Night with Conan O'Brien*. This flirtation with a career outside music echoed the work of his father, quipped Weinberg: "My dad wasn't a very good lawyer. He thought the law was sacred and something that was meant to help people. He didn't charge people like he should have… which is why I was allowed to play bars and strip joints when I was 14."

Van Zandt was already busy doing his own thing, of course. He collaborated with Southside Johnny & The Asbury Jukes, as well as with Ronnie Spector and Gary U.S. Bonds, and much later – in the 2000s, in fact – became an actor, delivering the role of Silvio Dante in what is regarded by many as the finest TV drama ever filmed, *The Sopranos*. He also got his own star vehicle in the Norwegian comedy series *Lilyhammer*, a fan favourite that spun off the Dante character in a Scandinavian setting.

Between 1989 and the reunion a decade later, Springsteen and The E Street Band appeared on each other's recordings from time to time. Four years after a *Greatest Hits* led to a temporary reunion in 1995, the full Springsteen and The E Street Band connection was resumed. The Reunion Tour was a huge success, as was an HBO special and live album, and life continued more or less as it had before the split in '89. A new album, *The Rising*, appeared in 2002 and everyone was very well recompensed indeed for the tour. The good times, it seemed, were

RIGHT Clemons joined The E Street Band in 1972 and was Springsteen's on-stage foil for over 40 years.

"I ALWAYS FELT THE AUDIENCE SHOULD LOOK AT THE STAGE AND SEE A REFLECTION OF THEMSELVES, THEIR TOWN, AND THEIR FRIENDS. THAT TAKES A BAND."

7:04 ★★★★★ BRUCE SPRINGSTEEN
BORN TO RUN

back: "When you learn a Bruce Springsteen song, it's like learning to ride a bike. You don't forget it!" chuckled Clemons.

In 2009, Springsteen and The E Street Band played that year's Super Bowl Halftime Show in Tampa, Florida, with a focus on each member of the ensemble, just to make sure the world – or at least, American football fans – knew that they were back for good. That said, the jobs that the musicians had taken during the Nineties had to be honoured, with Jay Weinberg filling in on drums at certain shows while Max recorded with Conan O'Brien, and Steven Van Zandt absent for a tour leg in 2013 while he was busy filming *Lilyhammer*.

Over the years, The E Street Band has changed its line-up, as members have departed the music industry – or this mortal coil – to the widespread regret of Springsteen's older fanbase. To them, understandably, the band isn't just a bunch of musicians; it is a concept, an abstract principle based on an image of older, safer times. When Danny Federici died of melanoma a year after stepping down from the band in 2007 to battle the disease, tributes came from far and wide. Charles Giordano took his place and was welcomed on board, as a veteran musician with a successful career behind him.

However, when Clarence Clemons passed away in 2011 after a stroke, he was less easily replaced, so embedded was his personality in The E Street Band: he is the figure against whom Springsteen is pictured leaning on the cover of *Born to Run*, serving as an excellent metaphor for his role in the group. For some, The E Street Band will never be the same again: we're fortunate that

TOP Springsteen and The E Street Band performing at the band's Rock And Roll Hall Of Fame Induction Ceremony in 2014.

MIDDLE A young Bruce and Steven Van Zandt sharing a mic while performing during the Born To Run Tour, 1975.

ABOVE LEFT On tour in 1985. "Nobody captured my audience's imaginations or their hearts like Clarence," Springsteen would later reflect.

ABOVE Since 2012, Jake Clemons has taken up his late uncle's mantle as The E Street Band's saxophonist.

"ONE THING IS FOR CERTAIN... I TOLD A STORY WITH THE E STREET BAND THAT WAS, AND IS, BIGGER THAN I EVER COULD HAVE TOLD ON MY OWN."

BRUCE SPRINGSTEEN
AT THE BAND'S INDUCTION INTO THE
ROCK AND ROLL HALL OF FAME, 2014

Clemons' music, along with that of his fellow musicians and indeed that of Springsteen, will remain with us on a permanent basis.

Clemons' death came three years before The E Street Band's induction into the Rock And Roll Hall Of Fame, when Springsteen inducted Bittan, Clemons, Federici, Lofgren, Lopez, Scialfa, Sancious, Tallent, Van Zandt and Weinberg, with family members representing the late Federici and Clemons. At the ceremony, Springsteen and The E Street Band performed three songs, although Lofgren noted, accurately: "They should have figured it out before the band started passing away. Clarence and especially Danny both took our exclusion hard, and neither is with us any more. So it was a bittersweet night."

The band were joined in 2014 by none other than Rage Against The Machine guitarist Tom Morello, as well as Clemons' nephew Jake. Tours followed in subsequent years, but Springsteen has alternated between using The E Street Band and other musicians since then. It's fair enough – he's under no obligation to tour with any given musicians – and in any case, he often promises that they're not done yet.

It seems that this particular band of comrades is here to stay, in spirit at least. Perhaps Steven Van Zandt said it best when he declared: "Rock'n'roll is our religion, and we will continue to lose disciples as we go, but we pick up the fallen flag and keep moving forward, bringing forth the good news that our heroes have helped create, their bodies lost, but their spirits and their good work everlasting."

As of 2021, The E Street Band is on hiatus along with the rest of the musical world: Springsteen has hinted at a tour next year. When that happens, we'll see you at the front. After all, there's a reason why Springsteen introduces them as the 'testifying, death-defying, legendary E Street Band!'

ABOVE Supporting The Boss' induction into the Rock And Roll Hall Of Fame in 1999. The band themselves were inducted in 2014.

LEFT Taking a bow after a New Jersey gig during the Born to Run Tour in 1984.

Images Getty Images

Released June 1984

BORN IN THE U.S.A.

Not just Bruce Springsteen's biggest album, but one of the biggest rock records of all time...

Over two years of songwriting sessions between 1982 and '84, Bruce Springsteen came up with no fewer than 80 songs, some of which went to *Nebraska* in acoustic form and some of which were reserved for the mighty *Born in the U.S.A.*. That's a prolific output by any standards – and when the latter album came out, Springsteen's profile went stratospheric.

What remains to be said about the song 'Born in the U.S.A.'? Like 'Hotel California', 'Bohemian Rhapsody' or 'Stairway to Heaven', it's more than just a song – it's a snapshot of a moment in time. The music may be simple, but it's powerful and assured, based on that famous ringing riff, while the lyrics are more complex, as has been evidenced over the last few decades by the number of people who fail to understand it.

Sure, that throat-shredding line of 'Born in the U.S.A.' sounds a touch jingoistic if you don't think about it too much, explaining its use in any number of patriotic, pro-American circumstances over the years. Dig deeper, though, and Springsteen's evocation

in the verses of the downside of life for a Vietnam veteran is clear: "Down in the shadow of the penitentiary / Out by the gas fires of the refinery / I'm ten years burning down the road / Nowhere to run, ain't got nowhere to go."

'Cover Me' follows up the obvious mega-hit with a subtler take on 'heartland rock', as Springsteen's music was widely labelled after this album, and it's here that you can really hear the mid-period Boss in full flow.

A common criticism of his songwriting and delivery around this time is that it's too masculine, too packed with testosterone and too self-consciously designed to whip up stadium-sized crowds. The cover of *Born in the U.S.A.*, essentially a rear shot of Springsteen in a singlet, his taut behind and a portion of the Stars And Stripes, somehow bore this out. It didn't help that he habitually performed in a headband and vest, toned biceps on display, legs akimbo like a heavy metal axeman, and bellowing in an elephantine vocal style that had become very much part of the package by the mid Eighties.

This, however, is unfair. A lot of the image was simply down to the styling of the time, and Springsteen's muscular performances – figuratively and literally so – simply reflected his passion and stamina. What's more, many of the songs on this album were calmer, quieter and less energy-packed than its opener, such as the beautiful 'I'm On Fire' – still one of the sweetest, most

wistful country ballads ever written – and the melancholic 'My Hometown'. Hit single 'Dancing in the Dark' brings a dose of pure, sugary pop in which Springsteen suggests that a life of urban misery will be leavened by a fun night out. As for 'No Surrender', it's among the most contemplative songs our man has ever written.

Thirty million album sales later, it's best to regard *Born in the U.S.A.* as a pivotal moment, both in Springsteen's career but also in American music as a whole. Heartland rock became popular, with homegrown social issues at the forefront of the songs; rock stars started going to the gym; and Levi 501 jeans, as sported on the album cover, became the legwear du jour. You couldn't make it up, could you?

LEFT Springsteen's notebook, featuring his lyrics to *Born in the U.S.A.* on display at Washington DC's Newseum as part of the Louder Than Words: Rock, Power and Politics exhibit in 2017.

MAIN The Born in the U.S.A. Tour of 1984-1985 remains the most successful tour of Springsteen's career to date.

TRACKLIST

SIDE ONE

1 Born in the U.S.A.
2 Cover Me
3 Darlington County
4 Working on the Highway
5 Downbound Train
6 I'm on Fire

SIDE TWO

1 No Surrender
2 Bobby Jean
3 I'm Goin' Down
4 Glory Days
5 Dancing in the Dark
6 My Hometown

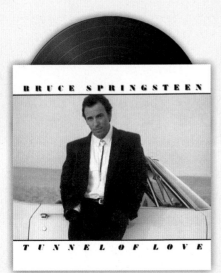

Released October 1987

TUNNEL OF LOVE

The Boss returns in '87 with his most 'Eighties-sounding' album. Wait, is that a drum machine?

Just as the success of 1975's *Born to Run* album had inspired the subtler, less energy-packed *Darkness on the Edge of Town* in '78, the monstrous impact of *Born in the U.S.A.* a decade later motivated Bruce Springsteen to dial down the intensity and come back with a calmer, more introspective suite of songs. *Tunnel of Love* was also written and recorded in the midst of Springsteen's split from his first wife, Julianne Phillips, and to add to the sense of loss that permeated the songs, he had also stepped away from The E Street Band for this album.

In addition, Springsteen was now interested in the studio technology of the era. By '87, a whole swathe of digital gimmickry was the order of the day in major recording studios the world over, now that processing power had increased to the point where computers could be useful tools. While it would be inaccurate to say that the new tech overwhelmed the new album, there's rather too much synth and drum machine here and there. Then again, hindsight is always 20/20, right?

You'd never know that *Tunnel of Love* was going to be a pensive album of contemplative songs from its opening track, something of a light-hearted quip on Springsteen's part. 'Ain't Got You' is partly acapella, although a Bo Diddley-style beat soon begins. The song is essentially the ironic lament of a man who has everything from fine art to fine women, but lacks the thing he wants most – the person to whom he is singing the song. Perhaps Springsteen was commenting wryly on the huge fortune that had come his way of late, leaving him bereft of a life partner as his marriage was falling apart?

The album does best when it dispenses with modern instrumentation and focuses on acoustic ballads such as 'Cautious Man', 'Two Faces' and 'When You're Alone'. On these songs, Springsteen finally makes it obvious why he was so readily compared to Bob Dylan in his earlier years, especially as he chooses to sing in a nasal drawl that is more Nashville than New Jersey. Here, the writing is sparse and subtle, allowing the vocals to dominate. Meanwhile, 'Tougher Than the Rest' is a lugubrious pop ballad that is not without its charms: Springsteen sounds surprisingly naive on lines like "Maybe your other boyfriends couldn't pass the test, but honey I'm tougher than the rest".

There is some gold in these hills, with 'Walk Like a Man', a slick, downbeat song that gets a bit synth-heavy as it closes, and the sweet waltz of 'Valentine's Day', a thoughtful way to end this patchy, slightly unusual album. Although 'Tunnel of Love' itself has a fairly

Images Getty Images, Getty Images/The LIFE Images Collection/ Brian Quigley (Julianne Phillips), Bruce Springsteen (album cover)

MAIN With *Tunnel of Love*, Springsteen embraced Eighties' trends: synthesisers, drum machines, and music videos with plenty of soft focus and slow-mo.

BELOW LEFT After the stadium anthems of his previous album, *Tunnel of Love* was far more introspective, thought to be fuelled by Springsteen's experiences during his marriage to Julianne Phillips.

BOTTOM LEFT During The Tunnel of Love Express Tour, Bruce and the band took to the stage as if they were fairgoers buying tickets for the titular carnival ride.

nasty hip-hop drum machine ruining the intro, it gets better as it goes along. Perhaps the album made its greatest impact with 'Brilliant Disguise', a warm, heartfelt song in the patented Boss style, and most of all with its video, a black-and-white single-shot clip that slowly zooms in on Springsteen as he sings, plays an acoustic guitar and gazes directly into the viewer's eyes. You can't help but admire the man.

TRACKLIST

SIDE ONE

1 Ain't Got You
2 Tougher Than the Rest
3 All That Heaven Will Allow
4 Spare Parts
5 Cautious Man
6 Walk Like a Man

SIDE TWO

1 Tunnel of Love
2 Two Faces
3 Brilliant Disguise
4 One Step Up
5 When You're Alone
6 Valentine's Day

Released March 1992

HUMAN TOUCH

How did the first of two albums released on the same day stand up in the grunge era?

Like so many musicians who earned their stripes as hotshot axe-slingers in the Sixties and Seventies – Paul McCartney and Elton John come to mind, alongside many others – Bruce Springsteen endured something of a torrid late Eighties and early Nineties, plagued by a lack of challenging material and an over-processed studio sound. His creativity was peaking, with a work rate that was second to none, but much of the music that he made was, sadly, a little uninspiring.

Witness the two albums, *Human Touch* and *Lucky Town*, released by Springsteen on the same day in March 1992. The rock world was in thrall to alternative rock, with Nirvana upsetting all received wisdom about the music industry in much the same way that the first wave of punk rock had done 15 years previously. What the kids headbanging to 'Smells Like Teen Spirit' needed like a hole in the head at that point was an album – let alone two albums – of slick, cheerful pop-rock, sung by a contented fellow in his forties.

Examples of pleasant but inoffensive songwriting on this record are easy to find.

'Human Touch' is slick, emotional pop, although it does get a bit more energetic later on, while 'Soul Driver' is very poppy, laden with synth and screeching lead guitar – it's all very *Top Gun*. Then there's '57 Channels (And Nothin' On)' a mildly enjoyable MTV hit thanks to its video, but still fairly cheesy, and 'Cross My Heart', which is just filler in the most forgettable pop-rock way.

'Gloria's Eyes' is more upbeat and catchy, but it's still very lightweight in a Bryan Adams kind of way, and when you've sat through the wispy 'All or Nothin' at All', 'Man's Job', 'The Long Goodbye' and 'Real Man', with its Huey Lewis-alike keyboard stabs, you've pretty much lost the will to live. Yes, 'With Every Wish' has a country vocal and guitar that makes a nice change from all the sickly pop, and 'Roll of the Dice' boasts some upbeat energy at last, but almost everything else slides by forgettably. Only 'Pony Boy' – a lovely acoustic ditty adapted from a traditional song – redeems the record with its heartfelt vocals and harmonica.

In retrospect, this album and *Lucky Town* were never likely to occupy a place in Springsteen's fans' hearts. The usual criticism of double albums applied to these two single records – that if you took their best songs and discarded the rest, you'd have a decent standalone album. Add to this the fact that Springsteen was now recording with session musicians rather than the fans' beloved E Street Band, and the die was most certainly cast...

TRACKLIST

1 Human Touch
2 Soul Driver
3 57 Channels (And Nothin' On)
4 Cross My Heart
5 Gloria's Eyes
6 With Every Wish
7 Roll of the Dice
8 Real World
9 All or Nothin' at All
10 Man's Job
11 I Wish I Were Blind
12 The Long Goodbye
13 Real Man
14 Pony Boy

MAIN On stage during The Human Touch Tour in Rotterdam, April 1993.

LEFT *Human Touch* had a mixed response from critics and fans; many felt the absence of The E Street Band was tangible.

Images Getty Images, Bruce Springsteen (album cover)

65

THE BOSS &
THE BIG MAN

"I'd searched high and low for years for a true rock'n'roll saxophonist... somebody who felt the music and the style we played in their bones." Springsteen on meeting Clemons, *Born to Run*.

Released March 1992

LUCKY TOWN

It was an unlucky break for our lucky man in Lucky Town. You really don't want to go there...

"I tried writing happy songs," pontificated Bruce Springsteen many years after the release of this flawed album, "and the public didn't like it." In this, he is only partly correct. The songs on *Lucky Town*, and on its partner record *Human Touch*, released on the same day, aren't particularly happy – they're just not particularly memorable, apart from a handful of relatively decent cuts. For example, the title track is a pleasant enough rock singalong and definitely not substandard, but since when was 'definitely not substandard' an expected assessment of a Springsteen song?

Still, let's be charitable here. When this album was released in early 1992, the Nineties as we think of them now – dial-up internet, PlayStations, Will Smith movies – hadn't really started, culturally speaking. For all intents and purposes, Springsteen's thinking as a composer, and the studio tech that surrounded him, was still very much stuck in the overthinking-it Eighties. Big rock emotion as we knew it around the *Born in the U.S.A.* era is definitely here, with 'Better Days' a rather overblown workout, 'Living Proof' an emotional rock song for the

devoted fanbase, and 'Leap of Faith' coming up trumps with a catchy chorus based on a satisfying descending chord sequence.

Where *Lucky Town* does better is when Springsteen has the sense to dial everything back and perform quieter, more thoughtful songs. A great example is 'If I Should Fall Behind', a calmer, pensive composition – always a musical direction that Springsteen finds easy to master. The same is true of 'Book of Dreams' – a somnolent song that is genuinely lovely in parts – and 'The Big Muddy', which is ponderous but interesting, with haunting slide guitar and Springsteen's echoed, partly-spoken-word vocals. 'Souls of the Departed' has a mysterious drone feel and beautifully layered vocals, and is an effective mood-builder, while 'Local Hero' is jaunty, quirky and basically a bit of throwaway fun. It has an amusing source, however – while passing a storefront, Bruce spotted a portrait of himself in the window. Not wanting to be recognised, he asked wife Patti Scialfa to go in and buy it. When Patti asked the shop assistant who was in the picture, they told her that it was an image of "a local hero," accurately enough.

As with *Human Touch*, often viewed as essentially the flipside of this record, this album ends on an effective low note, with 'My Beautiful Reward' a smooth, yearning ballad. Springsteen still knew what he was doing most of the time, evidently – and both this album and *Human Touch* have sold millions of copies over the years, so what do we know?

TRACKLIST

1 Better Days
2 Lucky Town
3 Local Hero
4 If I Should Fall Behind
5 Leap of Faith
6 The Big Muddy
7 Living Proof
8 Book of Dreams
9 Souls of the Departed
10 My Beautiful Reward

ABOVE LEFT Compared to *Human Touch, Lucky Town* was better received by critics, but many agreed that the dual release was a misstep.

LEFT The Boss played almost every instrument featured on *Lucky Town*, including bass and percussion.

MAIN Springsteen embarked on a world tour with a new backing band to promote both *Human Touch* and *Lucky Town* between 1992-1993.

Released November 1995

THE GHOST OF TOM JOAD

The 'New Bruce' era starts here – the moment where he transcended his rock roots and became a true troubadour

What do you do when you've become just a little too comfortable as a songwriter and your audience is getting restless? Why, you go back to your roots, and remember why you got started in the first place. If you're lucky and happen to strike the right vein of inspiration, you might just do what Bruce Springsteen did and score your most commercially and critically successful album in a decade.

Casting aside all thoughts of the *Human Touch* and *Lucky Town* era, Springsteen wrote and recorded 22 tracks in 1995, ultimately shelving ten of them for the sombre, understated *The Ghost of Tom Joad*. Seven of the songs are solo, with just an acoustic guitar and the faithful harmonica accompanying his gruff vocals, while five feature The E Street Band in full, if restrained, effect.

The album isn't exactly what you'd call a laugh a minute, but it certainly addresses important themes. The title track is the best known cut, and the song that addresses the topic of poverty in the American heartlands most fully. It's inspired by legendary folk singer-songwriter Woody Guthrie's song 'The Ballad of Tom Joad', itself a tribute to the 1939 John Steinbeck novel *The Grapes of Wrath* and its 1940 film adaptation. Readers familiar with the book will be aware of its stark, sometimes shocking evocation of life in the agricultural working class of the early 20th century. Many decades later, Springsteen's acoustic treatment of the subject is lyrically powerful, if also a little depressing to hear. It was covered by the protest band Rage Against The Machine in 1997, and Springsteen often played it when that band's guitarist Tom Morello was one of his touring musicians.

A similar tale inspires 'Youngstown', the dark saga of a real-life city in Ohio that was basically wiped out by the decline of the American steel industry. Springsteen sings the song from the point of view of a Vietnam veteran, and it's sober going, with very little to the instrumentation to detract from the vocals. The same is true of 'Sinaloa Cowboys', which has almost nothing to it – it's a masterpiece of economy. Meanwhile, 'Balboa Park' offers us some lovely fingerstyle acoustic playing; and 'My Best Was Never Good Enough' makes for a powerful end to this well-thought-out suite of songs.

Springsteen bagged himself a Grammy award for *The Ghost of Tom Joad* – proving that his original approach to music, a less-is-more blend of emotion and delivery, has always been where he shines most brightly.

TRACKLIST

1. The Ghost of Tom Joad
2. Straight Time
3. Highway 29
4. Youngstown
5. Sinaloa Cowboys
6. The Line
7. Balboa Park
8. Dry Lightning
9. The New Timer
10. Across the Border
11. Galveston Bay
12. My Best Was Never Good Enough

ABOVE LEFT Speaking about the album during its supporting tour, Springsteen explained: "I want to make a record where I don't have to play by the rules... have any hit singles or any of that stuff."

MAIN On stage in Brussels, Belgium, in May 1996 during The Ghost of Tom Joad Tour. Springsteen included older songs in his setlist, but with unfamiliar arrangements for solo performances.

CHAPTER 3
THE TIES THAT BIND

Images Alamy, Getty Images (main, family)

THE BOSS CLOCKS OFF

What does Mr Springsteen do when he finishes a show and returns to his private life? Let's meet the real Bruce...

You may recall the headlines that greeted Springsteen fans in the wake of his 2016 autobiography, *Born to Run*. It seemed that his revelation that he had spent many years suffering on and off from depression had astounded many a critic, judging by the number of column inches devoted to it.

"I was crushed between 60 and 62, good for a year, and out again from 63 to 64," he wrote. "Not a good record. Patti [Scialfa, his wife] will observe a freight train bearing down, loaded with nitroglycerin and running quickly out of track… she gets me to the doctors and says: 'This man needs a pill'."

Where did the affliction come from? Perhaps it lay in the Springsteen genetics.

In the book, he referred to family members with mental health issues, including agoraphobia and hair-pulling obsessions, which went largely unnoticed. "As a child, it was simply mysterious, embarrassing and ordinary," he remarked.

Readers who have taken the trouble to dig into *Born to Run* – an excellent, unashamed memoir by any standards – will no doubt have understood why depression reared its ugly head in Springsteen's life, and furthermore, why he chose to be open about it in his book. His early years, at which point he describes his family as "pretty near poor", were full of uncertainty and conflict.

It's interesting to note that Springsteen didn't recall his childhood as being marred by violence, although he did mention the alcohol-fuelled rages with which his father sometimes terrified him; instead, he talked vividly about having *too much* love and freedom. As a pre-teen, he was allowed to watch TV until the early hours, and he was showered with what he describes as an unhealthy amount of love from his grandmother. This matriarch, who had been bereaved decades before of a daughter – Springsteen's aunt – over-compensated with her grandson as a result. This over-attention made him into a spoiled kid who couldn't knuckle down to a school timetable, and because he preferred the company of his grandmother to that of his parents, conflict was inevitable, in particular with his father.

LEFT Sam Ryan Springsteen, Patti Scialfa, Evan James Springsteen, Bruce Springsteen and Jessica Rae Springsteen pictured together in August 2008.

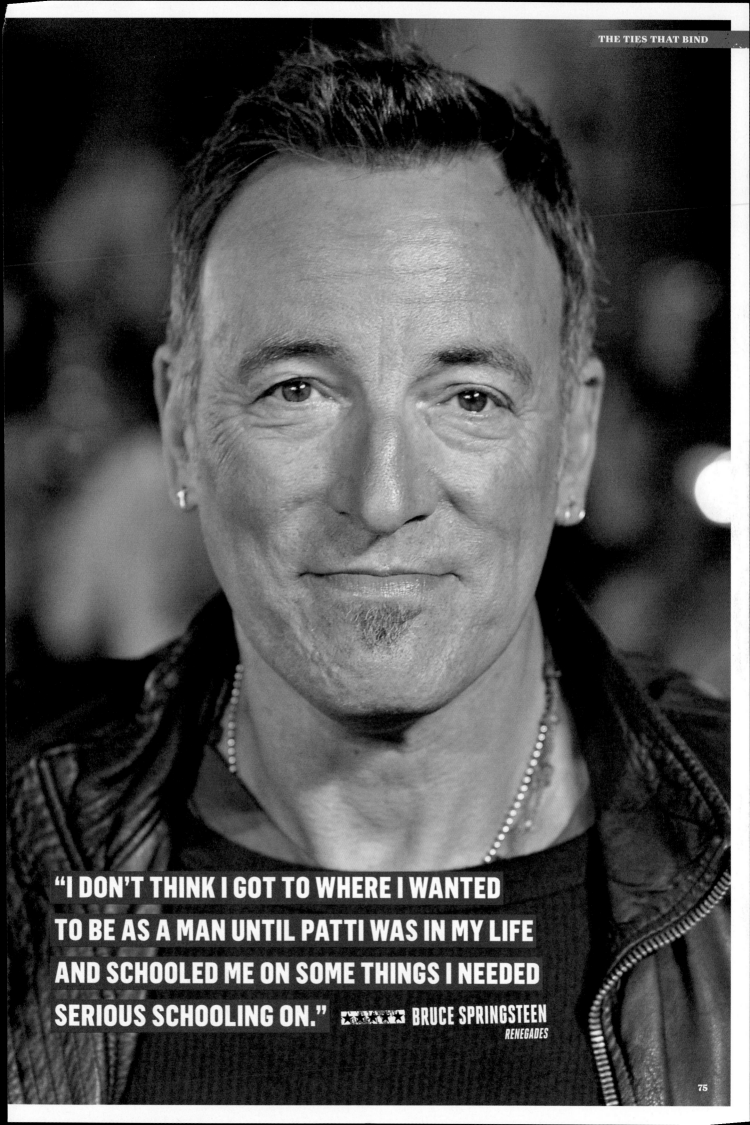

"I DON'T THINK I GOT TO WHERE I WANTED TO BE AS A MAN UNTIL PATTI WAS IN MY LIFE AND SCHOOLED ME ON SOME THINGS I NEEDED SERIOUS SCHOOLING ON." BRUCE SPRINGSTEEN
RENEGADES

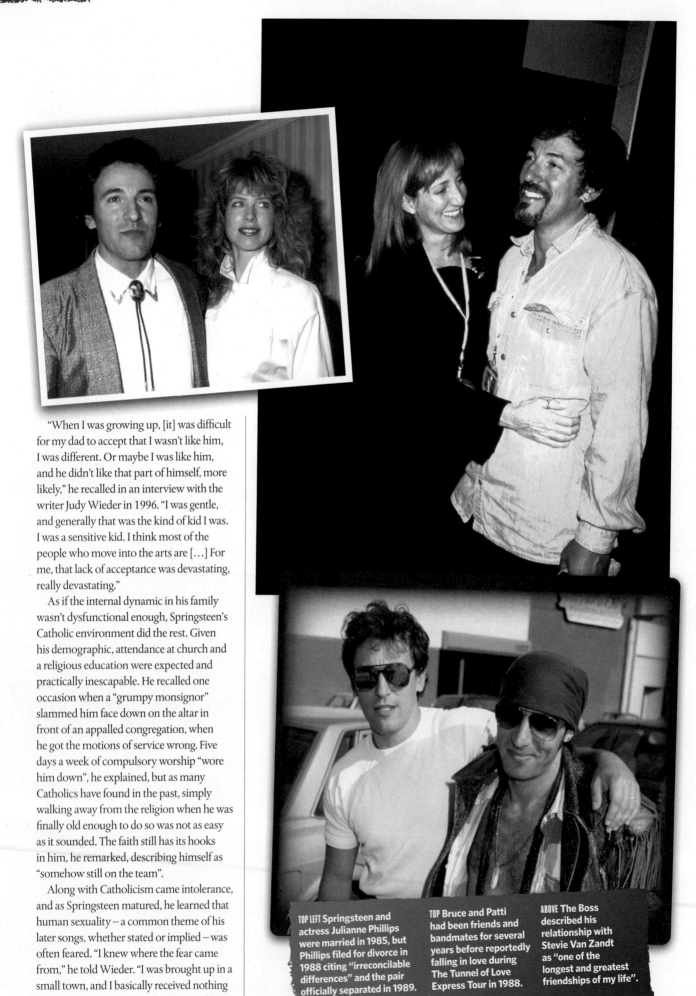

"When I was growing up, [it] was difficult for my dad to accept that I wasn't like him, I was different. Or maybe I was like him, and he didn't like that part of himself, more likely," he recalled in an interview with the writer Judy Wieder in 1996. "I was gentle, and generally that was the kind of kid I was. I was a sensitive kid. I think most of the people who move into the arts are […] For me, that lack of acceptance was devastating, really devastating."

As if the internal dynamic in his family wasn't dysfunctional enough, Springsteen's Catholic environment did the rest. Given his demographic, attendance at church and a religious education were expected and practically inescapable. He recalled one occasion when a "grumpy monsignor" slammed him face down on the altar in front of an appalled congregation, when he got the motions of service wrong. Five days a week of compulsory worship "wore him down", he explained, but as many Catholics have found in the past, simply walking away from the religion when he was finally old enough to do so was not as easy as it sounded. The faith still has its hooks in him, he remarked, describing himself as "somehow still on the team".

Along with Catholicism came intolerance, and as Springsteen matured, he learned that human sexuality – a common theme of his later songs, whether stated or implied – was often feared. "I knew where the fear came from," he told Wieder. "I was brought up in a small town, and I basically received nothing but negative images about homosexuality –

TOP LEFT Springsteen and actress Julianne Phillips were married in 1985, but Phillips filed for divorce in 1988 citing "irreconcilable differences" and the pair officially separated in 1989.

TOP Bruce and Patti had been friends and bandmates for several years before reportedly falling in love during The Tunnel of Love Express Tour in 1988.

ABOVE The Boss described his relationship with Stevie Van Zandt as "one of the longest and greatest friendships of my life".

Images Getty Images, Getty Images/Time & Life Pictures/The LIFE picture collection (Patti 1988, Van Zandt), Alamy (black & white)

LEFT Springsteen with his wife Patti and mother Adele at the MusiCares Person of the Year event held in his honour in February 2013.

BELOW A portrait taken backstage at the Stand Up for Heroes benefit in New York's Madison Square Garden, 2018.

BOTTOM After Clemons' untimely death in 2011, Bruce delivered a eulogy at the funeral, describing him as "my inspiration, my partner, my lifelong friend".

very bad. Anybody who was different in any fashion was castigated and ostracised, if not physically threatened. The gay image back then was the Fifties image, the town queen or something, and that was all anyone really knew about homosexuality. Everybody's attitudes were quite brutal. It was that real ugly part of the American character."

For his fans, of course, Springsteen's experience with Catholicism has been a gift, as it's inspired some of his most vivid lyrical themes and imagery. As he gained confidence as a musician and explored the depths of his psyche through songwriting, so his evolution as a man of faith ebbed and flowed, leading to rich veins of inspiration. This has also extended to his relationships: a four-year marriage to the actress Julianne Phillips was already failing as he wrote the *Tunnel of Love* album in 1985, leading to the melancholy tone of many of its songs.

It seemed that Springsteen's lifestyle as a travelling musician didn't exactly lend itself to stable family life, and indeed when he entered a relationship with his soon-to-be second wife Patti Scialfa in 1988, it's reasonable to assume that it worked out

more smoothly because Scialfa was a member of Springsteen's band. The pair first cohabited in New Jersey before moving to Los Angeles, where their son Evan was born in 1990; they married the following year. Their daughter Jessica arrived in late '91, and another son, Samuel, was born three years later.

By 1995, Springsteen was 45, a married man with three children, and one of the world's most prominent rock stars and activists. The spotlight was on him on a constant basis, and the media being what they are, criticism of his personal life was common. Of the chaotic years of the late Eighties, he commented: "I went through a divorce, and it was really difficult and painful and I was very frightened about getting married again. So part of me said, 'Hey, what does it matter?' But it does matter. It's very different than just living together. First of all, stepping up publicly – which is what you do: you get your licence, you do all the social rituals – is a part of your place in society and in some way part of society's acceptance of you."

TOP The Springsteen family, L-R: Samuel, Evan, Patti, Bruce and Jessica, at the Tony Awards in 2018.

ABOVE Bruce's stage performances in *Springsteen on Broadway* delved into his personal life between songs.

ABOVE RIGHT Springsteen's accounts of his experiences with depression have helped open up conversations about mental health, particularly in men.

One thing that society expects of most people – especially those of us of a certain age – is that we will lose our physical fitness at some point, becoming less energetic and less motivated to stay in shape as the decades pass and the sofa beckons. For Springsteen, this has never been an option, although in his early years, say before the age of 25, he was barely fit enough to make it through a gig. He has occasionally spoken of having bad habits as a young man, eating junk food and never doing any exercise, until he experienced an epiphany and changed his lifestyle considerably.

Hitting the gym and introducing a gruelling cardio routine, he built up his stamina to the point where he could perform his long, frenetic gigs at the energy level he desired. In the last decade, he has occasionally been seen working out at a public gym in New Jersey, saying hi to the few fans who recognise him but otherwise keeping his head down to focus on the treadmill or the rowing machine. One of his personal trainers described him, at around the age of 70, as having the muscle tone of a "hard tennis ball". Try pinching your underarm: can you say the same?

Asked about his interest in fitness, which went as far as outright muscularity in the Eighties, Springsteen told *Vanity Fair*: "If you want to get into it deeper, my father was built big, so there was some element of 'Okay, I'm 34. I'm a man now'. I remember my father at that age. There was the idea of creating a man's body to a certain degree. I suppose I was measuring that after my dad. And also, perhaps, in some way, trying to please him."

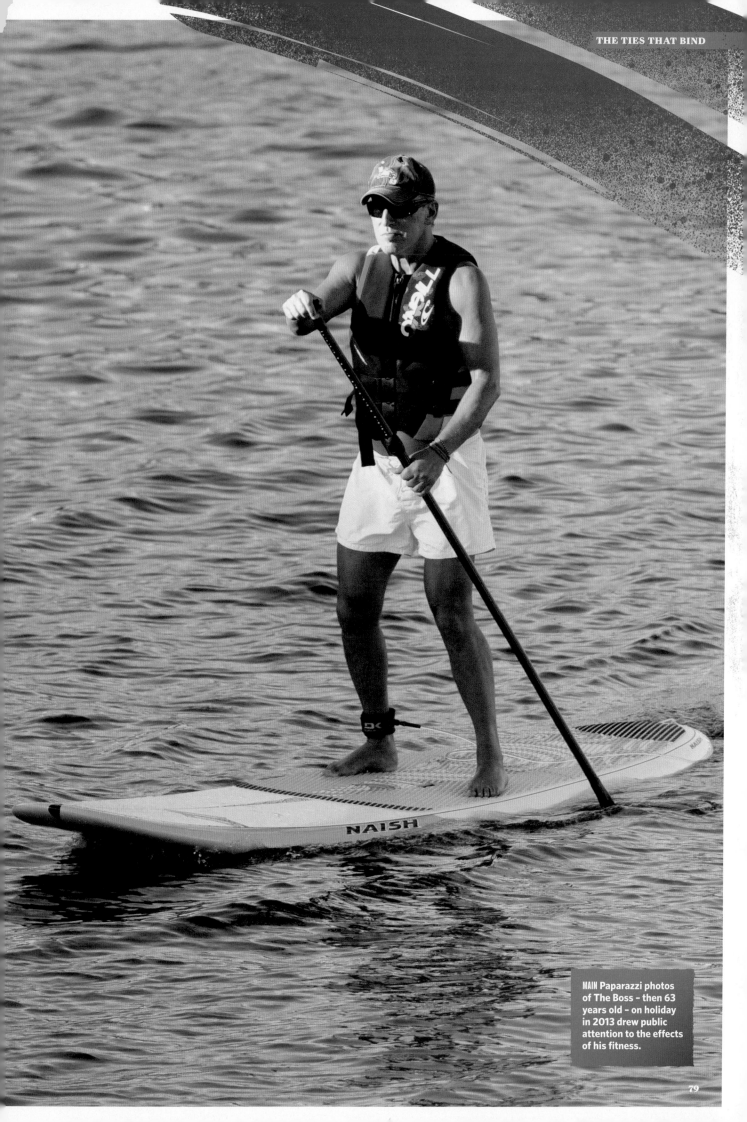

THE TIES THAT BIND

MAIN Paparazzi photos of The Boss – then 63 years old – on holiday in 2013 drew public attention to the effects of his fitness.

He added: "I also found that I simply enjoyed the exercise. It was perfectly Sisyphean for my personality – lifting something heavy up and putting it down in the same spot for no particularly good reason. I've always felt a lot in common with [the ancient Greek legend of] Sisyphus. I'm always rolling that rock, man. One way or another, I'm always rolling that rock." But it's clear his efforts have paid off.

The Springsteen kids have gone on to build successful careers. Evan, 30 at the time of this writing, is a recognised singer-songwriter; Jessica, 29, is an award-winning equestrian and showjumper at national level; and Sam, 26, is a firefighter in New Jersey. Perhaps their stability in adulthood can partly be attributed to their upbringing in rural New Jersey; their parents moved back to the Garden State from California after a few years, supposedly to escape the attention of the paparazzi.

It must have helped, too, that their father has a phenomenal work ethic; although this article is designed to explore Springsteen's private life, the ironic fact is that he is almost never off the clock, whether that means playing live, writing songs, participating in any number of socially beneficent causes or simply doing the everyday work of a successful musician. For this, we salute him; while depression and angst have always been part of his burden, as he revealed, he manages to stave off these ills in a wide

TOP LEFT Springsteen's daughter, Jessica, is a champion equestrian, pictured here at Winter Equestrian Festival in Florida, February 2021.

ABOVE LEFT Springsteen's youngest son, Sam, has served as a firefighter since 2014. He was sworn in to the Jersey City Fire Department in January 2020 (pictured).

MAIN Springsteen's eldest son, Evan, is also a musician. Father and son are pictured here together on stage during The Magic Tour in Barcelona, Spain, 2008.

ABOVE Springsteen, Patti Scialfa and Steven Van Zandt posing together in the early Nineties.

RIGHT Bruce and Patti have been happily married for 30 years. "We created a life and a love fit for a couple of emotional outlaws," wrote Springsteen in his autobiography.

range of positive ways, one of them being therapy, which he has practised for over three decades.

All this positive work has led to significant personal change, it seems. Stevie Van Zandt, Springsteen's closest friend in The E Street Band, remembered him as a reserved, timid character back in the Sixties, as he told *Vanity Fair*: "[Bruce was] shut down and closed in. You remember the grunge guys, with the long hair, staring down at their shoes? That was him. People were always wondering 'Why are you hanging out with him? He's such a weirdo'. Some people thought he was mental… [But] what inspired me about him, which nobody could really understand, was that he was completely dedicated. He's the only guy I know who never had another job. I had to do some other jobs and fight to do it full-time, where he was always full-time. I got strength from that."

The moral of this tale? Perhaps that the life of a wealthy, famous star is not as easy as it appears; there's a lesson there for all of us.

"DEPRESSION IS SOMETHING THAT HAS BEEN A PART OF MY LIFE. IT IS USUALLY OK, BUT LIKE CHURCHILL'S 'BLACK DOG', IT STILL JUMPS UP AND BITES YOU IN THE ASS SOMETIMES."

BRUCE SPRINGSTEEN
SPEAKING ON BBC RADIO 4'S
DESERT ISLAND DISCS, 2016

Images Getty Images, Shutterstock (Sam & Patti)

81

Released July 2002

THE RISING

Bruce Springsteen's considered response to 9/11 – and how that tragedy inspired him to write some of his best work in years

Almost two decades after the 11 September 2001 attacks on the World Trade Center in New York and the Pentagon in Washington, D.C., sufficient time has passed that we can view the consequences of those events with something approaching objectivity. The wave of support among Americans for their countrymen, the sorrow and anger at the loss of life and the hardening of their government's foreign policy aside, one relatively minor outcome of the tragedy was the re-inspiration of some of the USA's leading musicians in its wake.

As an artist who had commented for almost three decades at this point on life at all levels of American society, it seems inevitable that Bruce Springsteen would be moved to comment on 9/11. By the time *The Rising* was released in 2002, he hadn't released a studio album in seven years – and as for working with The E Street Band, it had been fully 18 years since he and they had recorded together. Famously, he is said to have been moved to write the songs after a stranger pulled up in a car next to his own,

wound down the window and told The Boss, "We need you now". Highly convenient as this anecdote appears, it seems to be true, as Springsteen recounted the tale in *Rolling Stone* magazine.

So what do we have here? You'd expect heartfelt music, of course, that considered a wide range of responses to the post-9/11 mood. Springsteen delivers this effortlessly on 'Lonesome Day', a call for calm and tolerance, and more hauntingly on 'Into the Fire'. Later he stretches his palette somewhat, adding a Middle Eastern flavour in the form of Qawwali singers in 'Worlds Apart', and loops vocals over a hip-hop beat in 'The Fuse', wisely placing himself on neither side of the ideological conflict. Mostly, though, *The Rising* is about direct calls for unity, with the title cut using a metaphor of human souls joining and

ascending together, while the plangent 'My City of Ruins' – written about Asbury Park, New Jersey – transformed into an obvious reference to 9/11.

The public were moved by *The Rising*, making it Springsteen's first to hit number one on the Billboard 200 list since *Tunnel of Love*, released 15 years before. The critics admired it too, awarding him the Grammy Award for Best Rock Album in 2003. Even the establishment got in the act, with President Barack Obama adopting 'The Rising' as his official campaign song in the 2008 election; it was also played at the 2020 Democratic National Convention.

That anonymous stranger was right: America evidently did need Bruce Springsteen at this fragile moment in the country's history.

TRACKLIST

1 Lonesome Day
2 Into the Fire
3 Waitin' on a Sunny Day
4 Nothing Man
5 Countin' on a Miracle
6 Empty Sky
7 Worlds Apart
8 Let's Be Friends (Skin to Skin)
9 Further On (Up the Road)
10 The Fuse
11 Mary's Place
12 You're Missing
13 The Rising
14 Paradise
15 My City of Ruins

LEFT The band's back together, L-R: Lofgren, Weinberg, Clemons, Springsteen, Van Zandt, Scialfa and Tallent at Shea Stadium in 2003.

MAIN On stage during The Rising Tour in 2002. The album was an attempt to reflect America's grief, fears and hopes in the aftermath of tragedy.

Released April 2005

DEVILS & DUST

Wake up – and *don't* smell the coffee – was the message on Springsteen's third acoustic album

Here's a terrible idea if you're a major coffee retailer, perhaps the biggest on the planet: ask a major musician, who has written scathingly about the corporate world for years, if you can release his album with your brand on it. This idea was taken up a couple of years after Bruce Springsteen released *Devils & Dust* by Prince, whose album *Planet Earth* was released in the UK in an issue of the renowned humanitarian publication *The Mail on Sunday*… This approach wasn't going to fly with Bruce Springsteen, though: remember, this particular rock star bucks trends.

In any case, *Devils & Dust* wouldn't quite have worked as a release in a high-street outlet. Here, on his third acoustic album, Springsteen addressed matters sexual in as explicit a manner as he'd ever done, specifically on the song 'Reno', which tells the story of a liaison with a prostitute in surprising detail. Elsewhere, The Boss invoked the usual heavy themes – the human condition and the choices that come with it, for example, on the title track. Loading his lyrics with rich images of divinity, death and mortality, Springsteen entranced his listeners one more time, with that opening song receiving three of the album's five Grammy nominations.

As with his previous acoustic albums, Springsteen adapted his homegrown New Jersey accent into a full country Tennessee drawl here and there, specifically on the excellent 'All the Way Home'. If you can get over this – and you should because it's fairly inoffensive – you'll enjoy the full-featured 'Long Time Comin'', which may be acoustic in theory but has the full accompaniment of a band in practice. More laid-back vibes await in the form of 'Maria's Bed', on which Springsteen delivers a falsetto vocal, which sounds much better in music than it does on paper, especially when juxtaposed against a honeyed mandolin.

The real depth of *Devils & Dust* comes with weightier songs, such as 'Jesus Was an Only Son', on which he intones considered thoughts about mankind's relationship with the divine, and on 'The Hitter', an older song where he allows a dark, Tom Waits-alike mutter to enter his vocal performance. The album benefits from both of these understated approaches.

Is it Springsteen's best record? Probably not; it's too introspective and countrified for that. But is it his best acoustic album? That's certainly possible: as a collection of roots songs, it stands tall alongside everything he's done, especially if you're in the mood to step away from stadium-sized rock for a while.

TRACKLIST

1 Devils & Dust
2 All the Way Home
3 Reno
4 Long Time Comin'
5 Black Cowboys
6 Maria's Bed
7 Silver Palomino
8 Jesus Was an Only Son
9 Leah
10 The Hitter
11 All I'm Thinkin' About
12 Matamoros Banks

LEFT During the Devils & Dust Tour, Springsteen played a variety of instruments, including the banjo, ukulele, piano and pump organ.

MAIN Springsteen performed alone during the Devils & Dust Tour, with a largely acoustic set.

Images: Getty Images, Bruce Springsteen (album cover)

FEBRUARY 2009
Springsteen and The E Street Band performing at the Super Bowl XLIII Halftime Show to an audience of 98.7 million viewers – a record at the time.

Released April 2006

WE SHALL OVERCOME: THE SEEGER SESSIONS

Paying tribute to one of the greats of folk music, Bruce Springsteen delivered an unorthodox covers album

From *The Rising*, inspired by an American tragedy, via *Devils & Dust*, inspired by American sounds, to *We Shall Overcome: The Seeger Sessions*, inspired by American socio-political history, Bruce Springsteen was clearly in something of a tributary mood to his home country in his fourth decade as a recording artist. He chose wisely when he recorded this album of songs made popular – rather than written – by the folk icon Pete Seeger.

Had he chosen to interpret the music of a country artist, say Johnny Cash, people would have found it predictable; had he chosen to record rock'n'roll covers – *Springsteen Does Elvis*, perhaps – he would simply have been retreading the ground he already covered in his live shows. No, Seeger's oeuvre was perfect for reworkings by The Boss, both musically and politically. The music industry agreed, awarding him a Grammy for Best Traditional Folk Album in 2007. What's more, Seeger himself thoroughly approved of the whole idea, as indeed he would.

Recorded at Springsteen's farm in Colts Neck, New Jersey, a lot of the songs are loose, rambunctious and a lot of fun. Some are more considered – see the majestic 'Shenandoah' – but by and large, the mood is not entirely sombre. The band, a group dubbed The Seeger Sessions Band out of convenience, do a great job of laying down a thunderous country-rock racket when required, but also know how and when to back off and leave their leader to do his job. Often, this job means him drawling the lyrics in such a hillbilly manner that it's hard to decipher the words – but then again, that's nothing new.

The point of this album may have been to celebrate a particularly important musical genre, but in the case of songs such as 'Old Dan Tucker' and 'Froggie Went A-Courtin'', you'd be forgiven for assuming that the album was intended as a suite of drinking songs, so rabble-rousing is their tone. Of course, the immortal 'We Shall Overcome' is not to be trifled with, and indeed Springsteen does no such thing, delivering a respectful rendition of the original protest song. A choir anchors the ethereal bonus 'How Can I Keep From Singing?', while the special edition bonus track 'How Can a Poor Man Stand Such Times and Live?' has more in common with old-school Boss rockers such as 'Born to Run' than any folk standard.

DualDisc and *American Land*-branded versions of this album expanded the tracklist and the record's incentive to buy, and the faithful lined up to do so – although you can imagine that, by now, more than a few Springsteen fans were yearning for a return to full-on rock. Fortunately for them, that was not long coming.

TRACKLIST

1. Old Dan Tucker
2. Jesse James
3. Mrs. McGrath
4. O Mary Don't You Weep
5. John Henry
6. Erie Canal
7. Jacob's Ladder
8. My Oklahoma Home
9. Eyes on the Prize
10. Shenandoah
11. Pay Me My Money Down
12. We Shall Overcome
13. Froggie Went A-Courtin'

MAIN Barnstorming with The Seeger Sessions Band during the We Shall Overcome Tour in the Netherlands, May 2006.

TOP RIGHT Springsteen pictured with prolific folk singer-songwriter Pete Seeger (1919-2014) backstage at a benefit concert in 2009.

ABOVE Performing at the New Orleans Jazz & Heritage Festival in April 2006, at the start of The Seeger Sessions Band Tour.

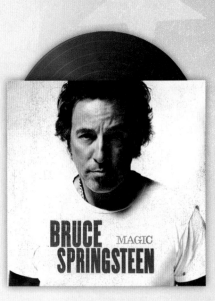

Released September 2007

MAGIC

With his most mature work in years, Bruce Springsteen worked magic for his followers in 2007

There's nothing like a good producer to add polish to an album, and in the case of 2007's *Magic*, Brendan O'Brien assisted Bruce Springsteen ably – just as he'd done with *The Rising* and *Devils & Dust*. The mention of O'Brien is doubly relevant here because he had history with a whole list of hard-rock bands of recent times, notably Pearl Jam, whose powerful, layered sound is all over this record. Just check out the opening cut, 'Radio Nowhere' for evidence – and notice also how comfortable Springsteen sounds on this song, loaded as it is with dense guitar. His country whine is absent for once; instead, he inhabits a full-chested range that suits the mood perfectly.

Not that Springsteen had abandoned his signature E Street Band sound – far from it. As Clarence Clemons, Garry Tallent, Max Weinberg and the rest of the gang flew in and out between their other commitments, he and O'Brien assembled a classic-sounding sax-plus-guitar-and-glockenspiel approach that sent shivers down the spine. Some of his lyrical sentiments were a little abrasive – "I'll cut you in half when you're smiling ear

to ear" he promised on the title cut – but by and large the mood was optimistic and the approach forward-looking.

If it's a cheerful, even jaunty, song you're looking for, try 'Girls in Their Summer Clothes' on for size. Here The Boss sings in a straight, clear tone that is so far removed from the nasal Bob Dylan squeak of former albums that it's barely recognisable. Note that the song is sung from the perspective of the 57-year-old Springsteen, so he sings – both wisely and accurately – of the titular girls walking right past him while ignoring him utterly.

Other songs are less optimistic. Take 'Gypsy Biker', for example, which is the tale of an American soldier who meets his maker in Iraq, and 'Last to Die', which may – or may not, depending on who you consult – be about the Vietnam War, and specifically a 1971 speech by the future Presidential candidate John Kerry. Finally, there's a bittersweet hidden track called 'Terry's Song': this piano-led stroll down a memory lane of friendship is dedicated to Springsteen's assistant Terry Magovern, who passed away in July 2007.

Magic is one of those albums in an artist's catalogue that turns out to be unexpectedly good despite a lack of hype before or after its release. Critics don't often reference it; 'Greatest Albums Of All Time' lists don't include it; and the artist themselves didn't release it during their imperial phase. Fans know the truth, though.

TRACKLIST

1 Radio Nowhere
2 You'll Be Comin' Down
3 Livin' in the Future
4 Your Own Worst Enemy
5 Gypsy Biker
6 Girls in Their Summer Clothes
7 I'll Work for Your Love
8 Magic
9 Last to Die
10 Long Walk Home
11 Devil's Arcade
12 Terry's Song [Hidden track]

LEFT Springsteen and Federici during the Magic Tour in Boston, 2007.

MAIN *Magic* became Springsteen's eighth number-one album in the US.

LEFT Reflecting on being part of an integrated band in the '70s, Springsteen said, "There was an idealism in our partnership where I always felt our audience looked at us and saw the America that they wanted."

ABOVE The Obamas and the Springsteens have become good friends over the years, after meeting during Barack Obama's presidential campaign in 2008.

HE SHALL OVERCOME

Activist, political commentator, participator in charity events – even a guest of presidents – Bruce Springsteen is a force for good

It would have been all too easy for Bruce Springsteen to have taken the millions he had made by the end of the Eighties, bought an island in the Caribbean – or, more likely given his preferences, off the Jersey Shore – and spent the rest of his life sipping cocktails on the beach. However, as we've seen, his experiences of poverty as a kid, his struggles to make it as a musician, and most of all, his observations of the unbalanced state of the American nation when it comes to poverty and equality, make that choice an unlikely one.

Essentially, Springsteen is a keen advocate for left-wing, arguably socialist values, a difficult stance to adopt in the cynical, modern world. It doesn't help, unfortunately, that he speaks from a position of immense – if duly earned – wealth. In the spring of 2021, Springsteen hosted an eight-part podcast with the former president Barack Obama, an ally for over a decade. The podcast, titled *Renegades: Born in the USA*, attracted some criticism, with one reviewer writing – harshly perhaps, but accurately – "If, like the former President and the Boss, you've been spotted off the coast of Tahiti, lunching with Oprah Winfrey and Tom Hanks on David Geffen's $300-million

superyacht, your claim to the mantle 'renegade' must be rescinded. The same law applies if you've been in possession of the nuclear codes, or starred in a Super Bowl commercial for Jeep."

Does this mean that the will towards true equality – not just in wealth terms, but in equality of opportunity – can only be expressed by the disenfranchised and the downtrodden? It's reasonable to disagree with that view, and in any case, Springsteen can justifiably claim to have begun his life close to the bottom of the pyramid of opportunity. It's more charitable to suggest that as soon as he was able to make a difference, he did so.

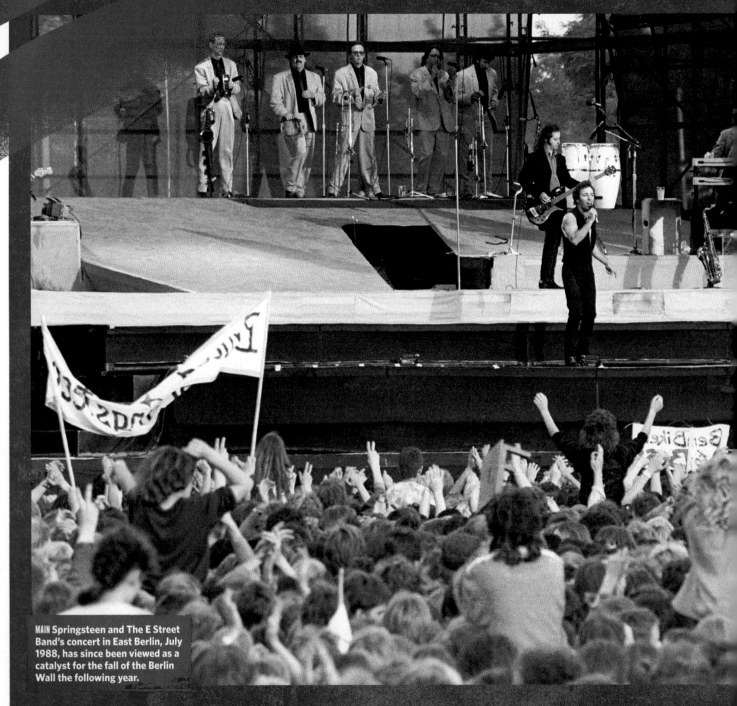

MAIN Springsteen and The E Street Band's concert in East Berlin, July 1988, has since been viewed as a catalyst for the fall of the Berlin Wall the following year.

Springsteen's career has featured a long list of activist ventures, motivated by the difficult circumstances of his own early life. Looking back on his childhood, he wrote that his father had been 'emasculated' by unemployment, leading the junior Springsteen to a keener awareness of how economic hardships hit the poorest people hardest. "My work has always been about judging the distance between American reality and the American Dream," he once stated, accurately expressing the balance between criticism and nostalgia that his music has always addressed.

As the years passed, he campaigned for environmental causes – the anti-

nuclear movement in particular, which started life as two Musicians United For Safe Energy concerts on 22 and 23 September 1979, which were filmed and released as *No Nukes*. As early as 1981, Springsteen began raising money for the Vietnam Veterans of America Foundation (VVAF), inspired by the veteran soldier Ron Kovic's book, *Born on the Fourth of July*, later made into a major Hollywood film. A single show that year raised $100,000 for the VVAF, indicating the potential of Springsteen's power to raise funds, even at that early point in his career.

A longstanding commitment to food banks began in 1984, when a United Steelworkers of America union

president introduced Springsteen to the Steelworkers Food Bank charity. To this day, he asks his followers to donate to these community food stores. Like many musicians of his generation, he took part in the We Are The World project in 1985, a truly sugary song that nonetheless helped to raise awareness of famine in Africa. Springsteen also performed for international organisations such as Amnesty International, for whose benefit he performed the major Human Rights Now! tour in 1988.

This doesn't mean that he took his eye off smaller, local issues. He has personally become involved in causes that probably would not have made the

LEFT As part of the supergroup USA for Africa, Springsteen recorded the charity single 'We Are the World', raising millions for famine-hit areas of Africa.

BELOW During his 1985 concerts in Toronto, The Boss encouraged fans to donate to the Daily Bread Food Bank, founded by Sister Marie Tremblay (pictured). He donated over $33,000, and fans raised another $4,000.

RIGHT Springsteen with Elvis Costello and Diana Krall at an annual dinner in aid of the Kristen Ann Carr Fund, April 2007. Kristen was the daughter of Springsteen's co-manager, Barbara Carr, and died of sarcoma in 1993.

"OUR TRAVELS AND POSITION WOULD ALLOW US TO SUPPORT, AT THE GRASSROOTS LEVEL, THE CITIZENS WHO'D BEEN SHUFFLED TO THE MARGINS OF AMERICAN LIFE."

BRUCE SPRINGSTEEN
ON THE BAND'S SUPPORT OF FOOD BANKS, *BORN TO RUN*

national press without his presence. In 1985, he and the country singer Willie Nelson took out adverts in four newspapers, urging the 3M Company to reconsider its plans to ditch 450 of its workers at a factory in Freehold, New Jersey, where Springsteen had grown up. The 25-year-old plant, which made magnetic audio and video tape for the entertainment industry, had been scheduled to phase out its operations, causing Springsteen to write: "Dear 3M: on behalf of the working people, their families and the community of Freehold, New Jersey, we urge you to reconsider your decision to shut down the 3M video and audio tape facility. We know that these decisions are always difficult to make, but we believe that people of good will should be able to sit down and come up with a humane program that will keep those jobs and those workers in Freehold."

On 8 November 1996, Springsteen combined social benefit with nostalgia when he played an acoustic set at his old school, St Rose of Lima, in Freehold. Only residents of the local borough were allowed to buy the $30 tickets, with the proceeds from sales going to a Latino community centre at the church associated with the school. He has also played several fundraising events at Rumson Country Day School in New Jersey, as well as appearing at benefit concerts for police officers and firefighters.

In 1993, Springsteen began to spread awareness of the sarcoma that had taken

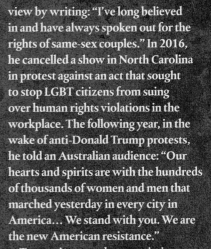

ABOVE The *No Nukes* live album and documentary film featured recordings from a series of concerts in 1979 organised by the Musicians United for Safe Energy (MUSE).

the life of 22-year-old Kristen Ann Carr, the daughter of his friends Dave Marsh and Barbara Carr. At the last concert of his Human Touch/Lucky Town Tour at Madison Square Garden in New York, he told the audience: "We're here tonight for the Kristen Ann Carr Fund. Kristen Ann was my good friend, and the daughter of my good friend, who died recently from a sarcoma cancer that not that much is known about. We're here tonight, we're going to be raising some funds so we can hire a doctor to study that thing full time."

In later years, Springsteen widened his focus to include gender politics as well as economic inequality. In 1996, he spoke out on the importance of gay marriage, and in 2009 supported this

view by writing: "I've long believed in and have always spoken out for the rights of same-sex couples." In 2016, he cancelled a show in North Carolina in protest against an act that sought to stop LGBT citizens from suing over human rights violations in the workplace. The following year, in the wake of anti-Donald Trump protests, he told an Australian audience: "Our hearts and spirits are with the hundreds of thousands of women and men that marched yesterday in every city in America… We stand with you. We are the new American resistance."

Trump, in general, was an irritant to Springsteen: he said of the then-president, "He doesn't have a grasp of the deep meaning of what it means to be an American," and later called him a "threat to our democracy." As he is a firm supporter of the Democrats, the Springsteen songs 'No Surrender', 'The Rising', 'My Hometown' and 'Streets of Philadelphia' were a feature of that party's 21st-century campaigns.

Note that Springsteen has generally avoided the urge to deliver political polemics from the stage, keeping his live shows dedicated to a community feel while encouraging people to donate to their local charities in a section of each gig informally named 'the pledge break'. Notable exceptions to this rule

Images: Getty Images, Getty Images/Mark Ralston/AP (Lincoln Memorial), Alamy/Warner Bros (No Nukes poster)

STAND UP FOR HEROES

A Benefit for the Bob Woodruff Foundation

IN THIS TEMPLE
AS IN THE HEARTS OF THE PEOPLE
FOR WHOM HE SAVED THE UNION
THE MEMORY OF ABRAHAM LINCOLN
IS ENSHRINED FOREVER

SUN CITY

ARTISTS UNITED AGAINST APARTHEID

FAR LEFT Taking part in the concert and comedy festival, Stand Up for Heroes, at Madison Square Garden in New York, November 2018. The annual event, held since 2007, raises money to support veterans.

LEFT Springsteen joined the Artists United Against Apartheid protest group, formed by E Street Band member Steven Van Zandt and record producer Arthur Baker, on the single 'Sun City'.

LEFT Performing in front of the Lincoln Memorial in Washington DC for the We Are One event at the first inauguration of President Barack Obama, January 2009.

first came on 5 November 1980 in Tempe, Arizona, a day after Ronald Reagan's election as President of the United States. Springsteen stated, "I don't know what you guys think about what happened last night, but I think it's pretty frightening. You guys are young, there's gonna be a lot of people depending on you coming up, so this is for you."

Four years later, the singer told his supporters: "The president was mentioning my name the other day, and I kinda got to wondering what his favourite album must have been. I don't think it was the *Nebraska* album. I don't think he's been listening to this one," in reference to the song 'Johnny 99', the tragic tale of a desperate man who turns to crime to escape imposed poverty.

Usually, however, Springsteen makes his political statements in his songs and to the press. Like Tom Morello, the guitarist from Rage Against The Machine who has often played in The Boss's band, he is now taken seriously by the left, mocked for his wealth by the right, and accepted as an elder statesman with something to say by everyone else. Whether Springsteen can ever achieve true democratic change remains to be seen, but dogged as he most certainly is, it appears that he'll never stop trying.

"THE E STREET BAND TRIED TO CREATE A SOUND THAT FELT AS BIG AS THE COUNTRY ITSELF. WE CELEBRATE WHAT'S BEST ABOUT THE COUNTRY AND WE CRITICIZE THE COUNTRY'S FAILINGS."

★★★★★ BRUCE SPRINGSTEEN
RENEGADES

LEFT 'Born in the U.S.A.' was originally recorded as a downbeat, acoustic track in 1982. The upbeat anthem we know today lends it a sarcastic edge.

Image Alamy

CHAPTER 4
LAST MAN STANDING

THE SPRINGSTEEN LEGACY

Musicians as influential as The Boss don't come along very often. Here's how he'll be remembered

Ever heard of an EGOT? The acronym stands for 'Emmy, Grammy, Oscar, Tony': the four major awards gifted to creative people every year for excellence in television, music, movies and theatre respectively. Coincidentally, it's the first four letters of the word 'egotist', but that's merely an amusing – if appropriate – coincidence. Only 16 people have won all four awards and thus attained the nirvana status of being an EGOT, among them Audrey Hepburn, John Gielgud, Whoopi Goldberg and Andrew Lloyd Webber.

Bruce Springsteen is not one of these hallowed 16 talents – but he's a whisker away from it, having bagged many Grammys, an Oscar, a Special Tony Award and, get this, not an Emmy win but an Emmy *nomination*. What's more, not just a single Emmy nomination, but three of them. On each of these three occasions he has failed to win his category, thus missing out on EGOT status. To you and me, this would probably feel like the most irritating near-miss ever, but to The Boss? Forget it. He doesn't care, having won dozens of other coveted trophies in his time – and also having sold 135 million albums and counting, let us not forget.

Put it like this, when it comes to Springsteen's recognition by various

industry and governmental institutions, it would be all too easy to make this article all about the awards he's scooped over the years. If he's put all of the following on his mantelpiece, let's hope that it's been solidly constructed…

Grammy awards alone would overburden the average shelf, with 20 wins out of 50 nominations. In fact, Springsteen has even entered the Grammy Hall of Fame, achieving recognition for *Born to Run* (2003), *Born in the U.S.A.* (2012) and *Greetings from Asbury Park, N.J.* (2021). He also won two Golden Globes in 1994 and 2009, and an Academy Award For Best Original Song for 'Streets of Philadelphia' in 1994. A nomination for 'Dead Man Walkin'' in the same category followed in '96, and he bagged

ABOVE The famous *Born in the U.S.A.* outfit on display at the 'From Asbury Park to the Promised Land: The Life and Music of Bruce Springsteen' exhibition in Philadelphia, 2012.

LEFT Dave Grohl, Sir Paul McCartney and Springsteen at the Grammy Awards in 2012.

"THE REASON I'M RUNNING FOR PRESIDENT IS BECAUSE I CAN'T BE BRUCE SPRINGSTEEN."

★★★★ PRESIDENT BARACK OBAMA
SPEAKING ON THE CAMPAIGN TRAIL, 2008

ABOVE Springsteen became a Kennedy Center honouree in 2009, in the esteemed company of actor Robert De Niro (pictured), director Mel Brooks, jazz pianist Dave Brubeck and opera singer Grace Bumbry.

ABOVE Steven Van Zandt's profile from his time in The E Street Band arguably helped him land his role as Silvio Dante in the critically acclaimed series *The Sopranos*.

the aforementioned Tony for *Springsteen on Broadway*, his 2017 concert residency.

When it comes to American Music Awards, Springsteen has secured four wins from seven nominations, including AMAs for 'Dancing in the Dark' and 'Born in the U.S.A.', both in the Favourite Pop/Rock Song or Album category, in 1985 and '86. The world of MTV embraced him early on in its existence, nominating him 11 times and giving him an MTV Video Music Award on four occasions, and even the literary world welcomed him into its inner circle in 2018, giving him the Audie Award for Best Autobiography/Memoir.

Springsteen's honours extend beyond his home country, with nine nominations for Brit Awards coming out of the UK over the years – although he's only won one, for International Solo Artist in 1986. Perhaps this is because his brand of Americana doesn't necessarily resonate in the UK quite as much as it does at home. Canada gave him a Juno Award for *Born in the U.S.A.* in 1986, and Sweden awarded him the Polar Music Prize in 1997.

Perhaps the greatest measure of any musician's influence is evident in the other artists who they inspire in their wake. If you tried to define the Springsteen sound – which is probably unwise, as his music has changed so much over the decades – then you'd come up with something like 'emotionally stirring folk, country and rock, often politically charged, with bittersweet nostalgic tones'. If that definition holds up,

there's a long line of Springsteen-influenced musicians to consider.

The most successful of these in purely commercial terms is Bon Jovi, also sons of New Jersey, and just as passionate about the Garden State as The Boss himself. Despite their career being a decade shorter than that of Springsteen, this hair-metal-turned-AOR band – by which we mean bandleader Jon Bon Jovi and salaried sidemen – have

ABOVE LEFT Jon Bon Jovi and Springsteen on stage at a benefit to aid victims of Hurricane Sandy in 2012. Both Jersey boys played at local venues such as Asbury Park's Fast Lane in their youth.

ABOVE John Mellencamp and Bruce Springsteen performing at a benefit concert for The Rainforest Fund in December 2019.

LEFT Bono inducted Springsteen into the Rock and Roll Hall of Fame in 1999, and The Boss in turn inducted U2 in 2005.

also sold nine figures' worth of albums. Although their sound was rather different to Springsteen's before 1995 or thereabouts, when they got rid of the poodle haircuts and spandex, the two acts have appeared on stage together at least a dozen times. Bon Jovi's songs often discuss the lives and loves of impoverished, struggling people – does that sound familiar?

The other Bon – Wisconsin-based folkies Bon Iver – also reveal some Springsteenian influences, particularly in the work of singer Justin Vernon, who has often expressed admiration for acoustic albums such as *Nebraska*. Then there's the Georgia sextet Drive-By Truckers, whose heavily countrified songs often tell tales of ordinary people dealing with the everyday afflictions that affect us all, such as infidelity, depression, addiction and warfare. Cheerful stuff, eh?

It's not always totally obvious, of course, that Springsteen has influenced a particular musician or band. Take two stadium-sized groups from the last two decades, for example – Foo Fighters and Kings of Leon. Neither band actively espouses an Americana-based worldview any more or less than many of their contemporaries, as such, but the emotional honesty of their songs, their widescreen dimensions

"THERE WAS SOMETHING IN SPRINGSTEEN'S MUSIC THAT TOUCHED WHAT I WAS GOING THROUGH, THE PROCESS OF FALLING BACK IN LOVE WITH MY AMERICA."

BRANDON FLOWERS
SPEAKING TO MTV NEWS, 2006

105

and the trajectory of the characters in the songs reveal a nod to The Boss. He's definitely in there somewhere, and when lead Foo Fighter Dave Grohl performed with Springsteen at the 2003 Grammys for a tribute to The Clash's Joe Strummer, the pairing made total sense. The same also goes for U2, who Springsteen inducted into the Rock and Roll Hall of Fame in 2005, after the Irish band had done the same for him six years before.

Still, check the legions of indie-rockers that have been the backbone of American music for decades now, and you'll see some very specific Boss references. There's The Hold Steady, whose 2005 album *Separation Sunday* is Springsteen-alike in both sound and subject; Arcade Fire, whose singer Win Butler has often referred to the Springsteen sound of his album *Neon Bible*, and has played with him on stage; and The Gaslight Anthem, another New Jersey band who offer their fans that instantly recognisable Boss feel.

Other subgenres of rock boast Springsteen elements, too. The Killers, whose huge hit 'Mr Brightside' you know whether you're aware of it or not, possess a huge Bruce fan in their singer Brandon Flowers, who sang 'Thunder Road' with him at the 2009 Pinkpop Festival. Then there's Badly Drawn Boy, better known as the timid British singer-songwriter Damon Gough, who also covered 'Thunder Road' and who wittily titled his 2006 album *Born in the U.K.*.

It's not all men, by the way: take Melissa Etheridge, for example, who claims that her life changed when she bought *Born to Run*, considers 'Jungleland' her all-time favourite song, and who also sang 'Thunder Road' – does no one cover any other song? – with Springsteen at an MTV Unplugged recording in 1995. What's more, it's not only winsome indie types who have embraced Springsteen into their songs: see Rage Against The Machine, the loud, sweary metal band who covered 'The Ghost of Tom Joad' and whose guitarist Tom Morello shares many a political conviction with his occasional employer.

Of course, we can't forget the passionate singer-songwriter John Mellencamp, considered by some to be something of a poor man's Boss for his take on middle-American lives and values, or Pearl Jam, whose singer Eddie Vedder has often sung Springsteen's songs alone and alongside the man himself. Finally, we have to consider *Sons of Anarchy*, the superb cable TV series that ran on the FX network from 2008 to 2014; its storyline of Shakespearean dissent within a criminal motorcycle gang has echoes of the Springsteen playbook, and the characters themselves most certainly deserve the comparison. Oppressed, desperate and riding fast motorbikes, the

TOP LEFT The Killers have cited Springsteen as a major influence. In 2020, frontman Brandon Flowers also interviewed him on the *Letter to You Radio* series.

ABOVE The 236-show *Springsteen on Broadway* residency earned The Boss a Special Tony Award in 2018.

LEFT Comedian and political commentator Jon Stewart is a big Springsteen fan, and has given speeches in his honour at several award ceremonies.

BELOW In an interview with *Rolling Stone*, Melissa Etheridge revealed that as a performer she often asked herself "what would Bruce do?"

ABOVE "I love Bruce Springsteen. He's the only friend I have that I subscribe to a fanzine about," said Rage Against The Machine and occasional E Street Band guest guitarist Tom Morello.

men and women of *SOA* could have come straight from the lyrics of *Born to Run*.

While we're talking TV, Stevie Van Zandt might never have been selected to play the part of Silvio Dante in *The Sopranos* without the success he'd enjoyed in The E Street Band – and when Springsteen himself played a cameo role in *Lilyhammer*, the *Sopranos* spin-off, the worlds of stage and small screen were united. Who knows how many fans of crime TV were turned on to Springsteen's music as a result?

After all this, what will Springsteen leave behind him when his time is up? The sales numbers, the physical awards in the bookcase, and trophies from various industry sectors are impressive enough, but more permanent – and perhaps more significant, depending on your point of view – are the lifetime honours awarded to him. The fact that he was inducted into the Rock and Roll Hall of Fame in 1999 and then the Songwriters Hall of Fame the same year was almost predictable, given his stature; what no doubt impressed Springsteen more was his induction into the New Jersey Hall of Fame – which didn't happen, for some reason, until 2007.

> ## "THE STORIES HE HAS TOLD, IN LYRICS AND EPIC LIVE CONCERT PERFORMANCES, HAVE HELPED SHAPE AMERICAN MUSIC AND HAVE CHALLENGED US TO REALISE THE AMERICAN DREAM."
>
> ### A STATEMENT FROM THE WHITE HOUSE
> ON SPRINGSTEEN'S CONTRIBUTION TO AMERICAN CULTURE AS HE WAS AWARDED THE PRESIDENTIAL MEDAL OF FREEDOM IN 2016

After three decades and more had passed and Springsteen was still firing on all cylinders, it became obvious that he wasn't another Kenny Loggins or Bryan Adams – in other words, an artist whose peak in the Eighties had been followed by a gentle decline into respectability. No, The Boss is too stubborn to fade away just yet, and also too creative, as his recent work has attested. In recognition of this staying power, awards of different kinds continue to come in, whether it's 'Born to Run' being named 'The unofficial youth anthem of New Jersey' by the NJ state legislature; a minor planet

LEFT Eddie Vedder has listed Springsteen as one of his influences. Vedder performed a tribute when Springsteen received his Kennedy Center Honors, covering 'My City of Ruins'.

BELOW Sam Fender cites Springsteen as a major influence; *Rolling Stone* have described the singer-songwriter as "Bruce Springsteen if he was a millennial from the UK".

"THE FEEL-GOOD MOVIE OF THE YEAR"

"IRRESISTIBLE... YOU WON'T STOP SMILING"

FROM **GURINDER CHADHA**
DIRECTOR OF **BEND IT LIKE BECKHAM**

BLINDED BY THE LIGHT

INSPIRED BY A **TRUE STORY** AND THE WORDS AND MUSIC OF
BRUCE SPRINGSTEEN

FOR ANYONE WHO HAS EVER WANTED TO DREAM. YOU'RE NOT ALONE.

IN CINEMAS SOON

discovered in 1999 being named '(23990) Springsteen' in his honour, or Monmouth University holding regular academic symposia on his work, and opening the Bruce Springsteen Archives and Center for American Music.

Does validation get any more serious than when it comes from your own head of state? In 2009, Springsteen received Kennedy Center Honors for his lifetime of contributions to American culture; in 2013 he was named MusiCares Person of the Year; and three years later he was given the Presidential Medal of Freedom by his chum Barack Obama, which brings us back to the beginning of this summary of his legacy.

Springsteen has spent his career criticising the many failings of his country, its inherent callousness towards its citizens, and its failure to evolve into a more equitable nation – and yet its establishment loves him. What does that say about his appeal? Simply that his work goes beyond anger and resentment, to a higher plane that people of all stripes can understand. That's a rare thing, and something to cherish.

TOP At the White House in November 2016, Bruce was awarded the Presidential Medal of Freedom – the nation's highest civilian honour.

ABOVE The 2019 film *Blinded by the Light* was inspired by the life of journalist Sarfraz Manzoor and his love of Springsteen's music.

RIGHT Some of Arcade Fire's tracks, such as 'Keep the Car Running', channel Springsteen.

Released January 2009

WORKING ON A DREAM

The Boss looks back to more innocent times... and forward to the challenges of the modern world

Written on tour in 2007-8, *Working on a Dream* was a solid hit for Bruce Springsteen, boosted by the title cut's use by Barack Obama on the campaign trail, a Golden Globe appearance, the half-time show of Super Bowl XLIII, and a VH1 documentary on the album. It debuted at number one on the Billboard 200 chart, reached the top of the list in 17 countries around the world, and tied Springsteen for the most US chart-toppers in history.

So what do we have here? Well, the eight-minute 'Outlaw Pete' is both the first and the most important song on the album. Despite its epic dimensions, propelled by an urgent orchestra and a definite Western feel, it's still as catchy as hell, with little pop hooks everywhere. Imagine keeping that upbeat feel going for so long; the synergy between artist, band and production team was definitely the secret sauce that made this song work.

The same optimistic vibe permeates 'My Lucky Day', with its upbeat wailing guitar and piano, and 'Working on a Dream' itself, a very mellow composition whose introduction hints at David Bowie's epic 'Space Oddity'.

You could enjoy more or less any of the songs on this record if you were in a cheerful mood. Throughout, Springsteen injects an effortlessly melodic hook into the vocal lines, for example in 'Queen of the Supermarket', which is nothing more than a sweet pop tune, with romantic strings and a restrained vocal from The Boss. This feel peaks on 'Surprise, Surprise', a thoroughly cheerful song, quite possibly written after a strong pot of coffee.

This being Bruce Springsteen, there are more serious elements to the album, of course. 'What Love Can Do' is robust rock, with the bass squarely at the forefront; 'Life Itself' is a pensive, heartfelt anthem; and 'Good Eye' is deeply thoughtful, with a distorted, megaphone-like effect on the vocals that reveals an ongoing experimental taste on the part of its writer. Check out the pure Fifties Las Vegas feel of 'This Life', with its very showbiz introduction, and the bonus cut 'The Wrestler', again with a swelling-strings intro, before Springsteen steps away into a bluff, acoustic strum. As for 'Tomorrow Never Knows' – surely a cheeky Beatles reference? – it's a thoroughbred country ballad, and delivered very economically.

If you felt that you had to point out flaws in this multi-faceted album, you might theoretically mention 'Kingdom of Days', which comprises bittersweet strings, piano and a passionate vocal – but which maybe suffers from too many 'I love you's. In addition, 'The Last Carnival' is a nicely restrained acoustic song, but there's a repeated two-note melody that you might possibly find annoying, as well as a country drawl on the part of Springsteen that is a little hard to take seriously.

But these are minor points. With *Working on a Dream*, Springsteen delivered a splendid suite of songs, beautifully rendered and produced. Was there much venom or vitriol this time round? Not obviously so, but that was to come later…

TRACKLIST

1 Outlaw Pete
2 My Lucky Day
3 Working on a Dream
4 Queen of the Supermarket
5 What Love Can Do
6 This Life
7 Good Eye
8 Tomorrow Never Knows
9 Life Itself
10 Kingdom of Days
11 Surprise, Surprise
12 The Last Carnival
13 The Wrestler

MAIN A portrait taken backstage at the Convention Hall in Asbury Park, New Jersey, where Springsteen and the band rehearsed for their 2009 tour.

LEFT The Boss and Van Zandt on stage during the Working on a Dream Tour in Herning, Denmark, July 2009.

Images Getty Images, Getty Images/Los Angeles Times (man), Bruce Springsteen (album cover)

Released March 2012

WRECKING BALL

You think you've seen Bruce Springsteen angry? *This* **is Bruce Springsteen angry…**

The Occupy movement seems to have inspired and outraged Bruce Springsteen in equal measure, as indeed it did for many. Capitalism has always inspired protest, but late capitalism of the early 21st-century persuasion is a whole new level of obnoxiousness: little wonder that with *Wrecking Ball*, The Boss took it upon himself to address a 'guy that wears a tie' for the first time, in his own words. The evils of Wall Street, the devastating consequences of the 2008 financial crisis, the raging inequality that paralysed so many Western populations… all were fiery subjects for discussion on this record.

The album starts with an inarguable statement of intent. 'We Take Care of Our Own' is loaded with martial drums, an air-raid siren guitar, and the usual Springsteenian tropes that audiences know and love – the plangent glockenspiel signalling the chord changes, heartland-of-America lyrical references to stir the savage breast, and so on. Do the lyrics express pride and solidarity in America? Yes, they do. Is it jingoistic? No, that's going too far. In this song, as with the rest of the album, Springsteen is drawing his loved ones close

in a time of conflict – his loved ones being millions of fans.

In line with the message of togetherness and strength, drums are all over this record, with 'Easy Money' a highly percussive country stomp, 'Shackled and Drawn' a beats-heavy blues workout, and 'Death to My Hometown' loaded with Celtic woodwind and choirs. 'This Depression' and 'You've Got It' follow suit. Is all this a touch over the top? That's certainly arguable, but the go-big-or-go-home sound is always a sure-fire way to gather the troops under a flag of solidarity, so we'll let it pass.

In any case, there's plenty of subtlety on this album. Take 'Jack of All Trades', for example, a piano-assisted croon aided by horns. The whispery 'We Are Alive' takes the same approach, building to an urgent peak, as does the title track, a love song to New Jersey. In two songs, 'Rocky Ground' and 'Land of Hope and Dreams', Springsteen steps some way into experimental territory: the former sees him duet over some

electronic sounds, while the latter includes beats that aren't quite hip-hop-indebted but go some way towards that sound.

The album debuted at number one in 16 countries and, along with its first song, was nominated for three Grammy Awards for Best Rock Performance, Best Rock Song and Best Rock Album. Did *Wrecking Ball* knock the capitalist elite from their perch? Far from it, but with this album, Springsteen at least took a damn good swing at them.

TRACKLIST

1 We Take Care of Our Own
2 Easy Money
3 Shackled and Drawn
4 Jack of All Trades
5 Death to My Hometown
6 This Depression
7 Wrecking Ball
8 You've Got It
9 Rocky Ground
10 Land of Hope and Dreams
11 We Are Alive

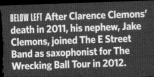

BELOW LEFT After Clarence Clemons' death in 2011, his nephew, Jake Clemons, joined The E Street Band as saxophonist for The Wrecking Ball Tour in 2012.

MAIN You'll like him when he's angry: *Wrecking Ball* was seen as Springsteen's angriest album to date.

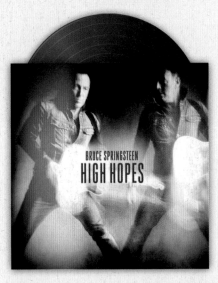

Released January 2014

HIGH HOPES

'Stopgap' isn't always a dirty word, as Bruce Springsteen reminded us with this collection of curios

"The best way to describe this record," said Bruce Springsteen of the covers, out-takes and reworkings collection *High Hopes*, "is that it's a bit of an anomaly, but not much. I don't really work linearly like a lot of people do." This was his way of explaining that the new album was made up of old and reworked music – not that he needed to explain. His fans understood that there was plenty of good stuff in the vaults; why not turn it into an album and release it?

Dive into the song 'High Hopes' and you're confronted with a Springsteenian anthem of the instantly recognisable type, loaded with big drums like the previous album, *Wrecking Ball*, and striking directly at the bolder emotions in the faithful. Fans of Rage Against The Machine will spot a recurring guitar bleep from that band's guesting guitarist, Tom Morello, which either sounds complementary or a little incongruous, depending on your point of view. The Boss is clearly up for a bit of audio experimentation on this album, including an unusual wah-effected bass on 'Harry's Place' and some curious electronic sounds on 'Down in the Hole', and why not? Few of his contemporaries would ever attempt such a thing.

Now, be aware that Springsteen does take the safe route on several songs on this album. If you're familiar with the slow build, the chest-beating passion and the nostalgic view of many a previous Springsteen hit, you'll be in well-known territory with 'Just Like Fire Would', 'Frankie Fell in Love' and 'This Is Your Sword', the last of which adds a layer or two of Celtic strings. These are not bad songs by any means, but they pale a little in comparison to 'American Skin (41 Shots)', a slightly unusual ballad, and 'Hunter Of Invisible Game', which is in waltz time.

Best of all, Springsteen – no doubt encouraged by Morello – delivers a reworked, full-band version of 'The Ghost of Tom Joad' that adds more dimensions to the old classic. Finally, his version of Suicide's 'Dream Baby Dream' is a marvellous way to close the album, played mostly on a pump organ before the band comes in: it's arguably the best song on the record.

High Hopes was also released in a deluxe edition that came with a DVD called *Born in the U.S.A. Live: London 2013*, a documentary of the British concert of the same name. It complements the newer material perfectly, as well as reminds us of the sheer weight of history that Springsteen was now giving us. Stirring stuff, without a doubt.

TRACKLIST

1 High Hopes
2 Harry's Place
3 American Skin (41 Shots)
4 Just Like Fire Would
5 Down in the Hole
6 Heaven's Wall
7 Frankie Fell in Love
8 This Is Your Sword
9 Hunter of Invisible Game
10 The Ghost of Tom Joad
11 The Wall
12 Dream Baby Dream

MAIN The Boss performing at the Concert for Valor, a Veteran's Day event on Washington DC's National Mall in 2014.

BOTTOM LEFT Lofgren, Springsteen and guest guitarist Tom Morello of Rage Against The Machine, who filled in for Van Zandt during the High Hopes Tour.

Images Getty Images, Bruce Springsteen (album cover)

WHO'S THE BOSS?

Springsteen and President Obama discuss various aspects of the American experience while recording the *Renegades: Born in the USA* podcast in 2020.

Released June 2019

WESTERN STARS

Go west, young man, advised the Boss with this cinematic homage to the sounds of the summer

By 2019, Bruce Springsteen had covered most of the emotions covered by the human species in his songwriting, from bittersweet nostalgia, via uplifted happiness and cast-down misery, to all-out indignant rage. Where else to go, then, other than somewhere in the middle of these extremes? *Western Stars*, which was accompanied by an excellent live documentary of the same name, expressed a kind of contented, dewy-eyed appreciation of California and its culture – or at least an approximation of America's sunsoaked west, from the point of view of rain-soaked New Jersey.

Springsteen called *Western Stars* "a return to my solo recordings featuring character-driven songs and sweeping, cinematic orchestral arrangements", which makes perfect sense when you give it a thorough listen. Your emotions will be stirred by 'Hitch Hikin'', on which Springsteen delivers a near-perfect Bob Dylan impression on vocals, with strings and piano adding to the heartfelt effect. 'The Wayfarer' with its thoughtful piano, does a similar job and is a welcome touch of observational

composition. The love story towards the pioneers of yore continues with 'Tucson Train', and with 'Western Stars' itself – all acoustic and lapsteel guitar – Springsteen goes full country, perhaps where he has always wanted to be.

It's not all whinnying horses and firepits under the stars, though. Springsteen delivers a cheery, if inconsequential, bit of whimsy in 'Sleepy Joe's Café', where he invokes the old faithful 'summer girls' trope, and there's 'Drive Fast (The Stuntman)', a thoughtful piano song that builds by its end to the usual widescreen landscapes. 'Stones' merges sweet strings and horns into a cinematic piece of work, while 'Moonlight Motel' is a lovely acoustic and strings stomp.

At heart, this album is an ode to the big skies and surf of American geography,

which means that there are ample opportunities for wide, deep sounds and observations. 'Chasin' Wild Horses' and 'Somewhere North of Nashville' are self-explanatory, while 'Sundown' gives us the opportunity for a major singalong. Little wonder that the film version of the album added a cover of Glen Campbell's immortal 'Rhinestone Cowboy', perhaps the ultimate distillation of this type of Americana.

Rewarding as the album is, it is perhaps better appreciated in the form of the

MAIN Both the album and the companion film of *Western Stars* were met with critical acclaim.

LEFT BELOW A portrait of The Boss at his home in Colts Neck, New Jersey, 2019.

LEFT BOTTOM Bruce has worked with director and film editor Thom Zimny on various projects over the years.

accompanying documentary film, also titled Western Stars. Directed by The Boss himself, with Thom Zimny, the movie is essentially a full performance of the album, enabling a closer look into the emotions and musicianship that the songs required to work as well as they did. The documentary premiered at the Toronto International Film Festival in September 2019, and a theatrical release came the following month. Fans understood the importance of the visual accompaniment to the record, and it was rewarded with high attendances, just before the world suddenly ground to a halt in 2020.

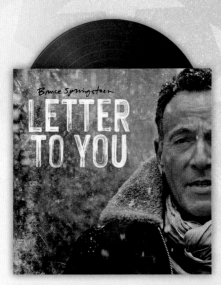

Released October 2020

LETTER TO YOU

Pandemic? What pandemic? When Bruce Springsteen decides to make an album, he'll make one, whatever the conditions

Recorded in just four days at Bruce Springsteen's home studio in late 2019, *Letter to You* was all set to continue The Boss's forward motion into his seventies in much the same way as its predecessors *High Hopes* (2014) and *Western Stars* (2019). That is to say, it was meant to show any doubters one more time that he could still make and perform meaningful, emotional music that had something important to say about life in the modern world. The new record did indeed fulfil that goal – but in the absence of in-person live performances or a world tour (for obvious reasons), its many qualities may have been lost in the online translation.

Let us attempt to redress that here. *Letter to You* is a clear demonstration that Springsteen and his music – even his signature sound – still have a place in the third decade of this century. A spell of writer's block was resolved when he found himself inspired by the death of a former bandmate, George Theiss (of The Castiles), which goes some way to explain the songs' themes of all things passing by. It's fitting, perhaps, that three of the songs – 'If I Was the Priest', 'Janey Needs a Shooter' and 'Song for Orphans' – were written as far back as 1973, given the record's whole-life perspective.

Springsteen expresses powerful emotions here, whether with restrained acoustic balladry – see 'One Minute You're Here' and 'Rainmaker' – or the full barrage of heavy-rock instrumentation, as in 'The Power of Prayer' and 'If I Was the Priest'. Occasionally he looks in the rear-view mirror for inspiration, and it works beautifully, as in the case of 'Burnin' Train', which suggests the sound of 1976 all over again, and 'Janey Needs a Shooter', an organ-driven preach straight from the drawer marked 'Like a Rolling Stone'.

Listen out for the guitar-heavy chunk of the title cut, complete with the audible

TRACKLIST

1. One Minute You're Here
2. Letter to You
3. Burnin' Train
4. Janey Needs a Shooter
5. Last Man Standing
6. The Power of Prayer
7. House of a Thousand Guitars
8. Rainmaker
9. If I Was the Priest
10. Ghosts
11. Song for Orphans
12. I'll See You in My Dreams

MAIN Bruce wrote much of the album after the death of former bandmate, George Theiss, and explores the themes of mortality and loss.

BELOW LEFT Patti and Bruce during a lockdown performance in support of the New Jersey Pandemic Relief Fund, April 2020.

BELOW Making a surprise appearance at the Light of Day benefit concert in Asbury Park, January 2020.

rasp of Springsteen's 70 years in his vocals; 'House of a Thousand Guitars', with its heartstring-twanging piano; 'Song for Orphans', which has a powerful harmonica melody; and 'I'll See You in My Dreams', where Springsteen disguises a mixture of emotions with a countrified sound that is both slick and organic. It's great work

throughout, a fact noted by the huge numbers of fans who bought the record.

The album was supported by promotional appearances on *The Late Show with Stephen Colbert*, *Saturday Night Live*, and on Ireland's *The Late Late Show* (to boost across-the-pond publicity). It was also accompanied by a five-part series on Apple

Music's Letter to You Radio channel and a full documentary on the making of the album, again hosted by Apple TV. The media loves Springsteen as much as ever in 2021, just as they should: who else of his generation is as worthy of their support? You know the answer.

Images Danny Clinch/Shore Fire Media (main), Alamy (Light of Day), Getty Images (with Patti), Bruce Springsteen (album cover)

WHAT'S NEXT FOR THE BOSS?

Bruce Springsteen has been busier than ever in recent years – and he's showing no sign of slowing down any time soon...

TOP "We've been sharing a studio, Bruce has just been so prolific lately that it's hard for me to get in there." – Patti Scialfa on recording during the pandemic.

ABOVE The *Springsteen on Broadway* performances were a combination of spoken-word reflections on Bruce's life, with acoustic versions of some of his best-known songs.

Now in his early seventies, Bruce Springsteen is fitter and more energetic than most people are at half his age. In the Eighties, certain members of the media made a sport out of mocking his musclebound physique and the boundless enthusiasm he exuded in his marathon concerts – but who's laughing now? At an age when most of us are too tired for anything more demanding than weeding the patio, The Boss is out there, striding the world's biggest stages and commanding as big an audience as he did back in 1986.

At least, he would be – if it weren't for the small matter of the pandemic. Forced to stay at home and refine his creativity within the four walls of his home, Springsteen is evidently refusing to laze around and do nothing, as we'll see in a moment. He's had a busy few years, and he plans to have quite a few more of those before he hangs up his Telecaster – so what's he been up to lately?

Looking back to 2016, Springsteen's most recent period of creativity effectively began when he completed seven years of part-time literary endeavour with the publication of his autobiography, *Born to Run*. Given the existence of a well-known Boss biography of the same name, he was asked by one or

two interviewers if he had considered a different, less predictable title. The answer was that he had indeed done so, but that the iconic three-word phrase simply could not be bettered as a summation of his life and career so far. "Man enters town, detonates; man leaves town. Just how I like it," ran one memorable line in *Born to Run*, espousing Springsteen's perennially itinerant lifestyle.

Fans and critics evidently agreed with him, lining up to buy the memoir on the nine-date book tour that Springsteen executed in the US, UK, Germany and Canada, beginning in a Barnes & Noble in good old Freehold, New Jersey. As the book hit number one on the *New York Times* Best Sellers list, a compilation album of his songs called *Chapter and Verse* was released around the same time as his book, making the publication even more of an event – but he didn't stop there, having set up a whole *Springsteen on Broadway* project for the following year.

While fans waited for this second phase of book-related performances, Springsteen had the small matter of a world tour to complete. In the midst of completing his publicity for *Born to Run*, he was also finishing off the immense River 2016 Tour, the top-grossing

Images Getty Images, Getty Images/NBCUniversal/Will Heath (SNL), Danny Clinch/Shore Fire Media (main), Spotify (Renegades), Apple (Letter to You radio)

LEFT Bruce and the band performing on *SNL* in December 2020. Due to Covid restrictions, it was reportedly the first time bassist Garry Tallent had ever missed an E Street Band performance.

BELOW LEFT Appearing on the video board at Boston's Fenway Park, Springsteen takes part in a rehearsal for the Dropkick Murphys' Streaming Outta Fenway benefit concert in May 2020.

set of live dates for that year: it brought in $268.3 million globally, an astounding feat for a musician of Springsteen's vintage. One of the dates, performed at Citizens Bank Park in Philadelphia, Pennsylvania, lasted a full four hours and four minutes, his longest-ever US gig. Sure, the tickets were costly – but how about that for value for money?

You may recall that 2016 was also a Presidential election year, and while the result didn't go the way of Springsteen's preferred party, the Democrats, it wasn't for want of trying on his part. At a rally on 7 November he played a three-song acoustic set in support of Hillary Clinton's campaign, and two weeks later he received the Presidential Medal of Freedom award by the outgoing President, Barack Obama. From a British point of view, it's interesting to consider the reverence in which such an award is held; just as our monarchy hands out CBEs, OBEs and knighthoods to individuals of particular skill or fondness for charitable donations, so the American President has the ability to ennoble people with this elevated honour. It is something to be taken very seriously, as Springsteen

evidently did, sending the Obamas off at the end of their reign with a 15-song acoustic set at the White House on 12 January 2017.

When *Springsteen on Broadway* kicked off at the Walter Kerr Theatre in New York City in late 2017, it was an immediate hit. The show's blend of music and spoken-word sections, whether from the *Born to Run* book or Springsteen ad-libbing stories from his career, was an immediate hit with fans – and its run had to be extended three times, such was its appeal. Eventually, it ran all the way until the end of 2018, introducing a new model of live performance that many other musicians have since adopted. The show won a Special Tony Award, and a live album of the same name reached the top 10 in many countries.

Into 2019, and it was time for a new Springsteen album: *Western Stars*, released in June. This time, the album was accompanied by a film of the same name, co-directed by its star and featuring The Boss and his band playing the new songs live. A soundtrack, logically titled *Western Stars – Songs from the Film*, was also issued, making the new project essentially a triple release.

MAIN Springsteen's 20th studio album *Letter to You* was released during the Covid pandemic in October 2020, and garnered widespread critical acclaim.

"WHEN THIS EXPERIENCE IS OVER, I AM GONNA THROW THE WILDEST PARTY YOU HAVE EVER SEEN – AND YOU, MY FRIENDS, ARE ALL INVITED."

BRUCE SPRINGSTEEN
DISCUSSING LIFE AFTER THE PANDEMIC
ON *FROM MY HOME TO YOURS*

LEFT Amid the pandemic, *Letter to You* was promoted with digital events like Apple's Letter to You Radio series, in which Bruce discussed his career with guest stars.

BELOW In early 2021, Springsteen and former president Barack Obama released their podcast, *Renegades* – a series of conversations about their lives, music and America.

"THE BEST MUSIC IS THERE TO PROVIDE YOU WITH SOMETHING TO FACE THE WORLD WITH."

★★★★★ BRUCE SPRINGSTEEN

TOP As vaccination efforts are turning the tide in the Covid pandemic, hopefully it won't be long before Bruce and The E Street Band are back on tour performing live concerts once again.

ABOVE Now in his seventies, with 20 studio albums and over 2,700 concert performances, The Boss shows no signs of retiring any time soon.

Then, of course, a rogue virus shut everything down for the world's live performers – and as you'll recall, it seemed at first as if the shutdown might last into the foreseeable future. We know now that things will normalise at some point, but as 2020 dawned and a year of dates was cancelled, Steven Van Zandt put it best when he quipped with typical bleak humour, "Let's just say I thought I was going to be busier than I am." Springsteen himself observed: "I'm going to consider myself lucky if I lose just a year of touring life. Once you hit 70, there's a finite amount of tours and a finite amount of years that you have [so if] you lose one or two, that's not so great."

Still, The Boss switched gears with alacrity, moving – as so many of us have done – to a largely online existence. In May 2020 he appeared remotely as part of a live-streamed gig by Dropkick Murphys. After a couple of years of these events, we have become a little jaded about online gigs, perhaps, but back then the idea of a streamed show was still novel – and in fact that single gig raised over $700,000 for three charities.

Working as hard as ever, Springsteen released his most recent album, *Letter to You*, on 23 October 2020. The title track and the song 'Ghosts' were released as singles, and the new release was supported by an

LEFT While speaking on his *From My Home to Yours* radio series in May 2020, Springsteen described lockdown life as "empty and unused time, I don't care for – especially at 70."

ABOVE LEFT Performing 'Land of Hope and Dreams' at the televised special for President Biden's inauguration in January 2021.

ABOVE Speaking with director Martin Scorsese about *Springsteen on Broadway* at the opening night for Netflix's FYSEE event in May 2019.

BELOW On Stage at Brazil's Rock in Rio festival in September 2013. The Boss played until 3am with a mammoth three-hour set... just days before his 64th birthday.

appearance at the end of the year on *Saturday Night Live*. Pandemic precautions and travel concerns meant that bassist Gary Tallent and violinist Soozie Tyrell were unable to attend. Regarding the former, supposedly this was the first of The E Street Band's gigs that the affable bass player had ever missed since the band was founded in 1972.

Springsteen also occupied his time during the pandemic with the aforementioned *Renegades* podcast with Barack Obama, and his own radio show *From My Home to Yours*, hosted on the Sirius XM channel. If there was one benefit to the accursed coronavirus for Springsteen fans, it's that we were gifted an intimate look inside the character of the man – one which might well never have arisen in normal conditions. Although he is yet to reveal many post-pandemic plans (including a rumoured 2022/2023 tour), Springsteen's insights into music and politics make both shows essential listening and viewing for anyone interested in his unique perspective.

We've said it before, but which other musician of Springsteen's age and demographic is attracting this level of support these days? Make sure you listen to him speak, and conditions permitting, see him play live. There is no-one else quite like him. Bruce Springsteen stands alone.

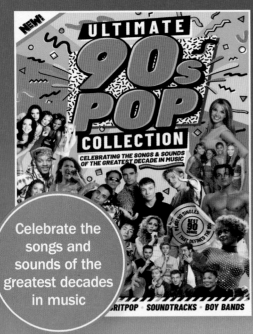

Celebrate the songs and sounds of the greatest decades in music

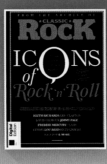
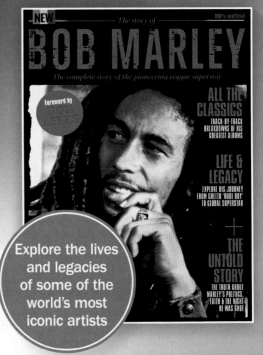

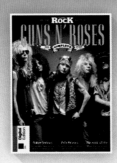

Explore the lives and legacies of some of the world's most iconic artists

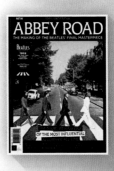

Crank up the volume and get to know the best rock and metal bands on the planet